Let Me Think

Let Me Think

J. Robert Lennon

stories

GRAYWOLF PRESS

This publication is made possible, in part, by the voters of Minnesota through a Minnesota State Arts Board Operating Support grant, thanks to a legislative appropriation from the arts and cultural heritage fund. Significant support has also been provided by Target Foundation, the McKnight Foundation, the Lannan Foundation, the Amazon Literary Partnership, and other generous contributions from foundations, corporations, and individuals. To these organizations and individuals we offer our heartfelt thanks.

Published by Graywolf Press
250 Third Avenue North, Suite 600
Minneapolis, Minnesota 55401

www.graywolfpress.org

Published in the United States of America

ISBN 978-1-64445-049-9

2 4 6 8 9 7 5 3 1
First Graywolf Printing, 2021

Library of Congress Control Number: 2020937702

Cover design: Kyle G. Hunter

Contents

ONE

TWO

THREE

Let Me Think

ONE

Girls

The girls don't want to be seen, except when they want to be seen, at which time they are easy to find. But when they don't want to be seen, which is usually, to find one is rare. A visitor who knows about the girls, and believes that their ability to conceal themselves has been overstated, will sometimes see one who wants to be seen and announce, not without a certain smugness, that he has seen one of the supposedly elusive girls, and that there isn't much to their storied invisibility after all, is there. But then the visitor will be told, sometimes by the girl herself, that she was not, in fact, hidden; and the visitor will scoff, and then the girl will vanish.

Of course the girls aren't really invisible. They are merely skilled at concealment. The tactics they employ are known to include but are likely not limited to:

- blending into backgrounds
- extreme stillness
- stealthy wardrobe changes
- strategic irrelevance
- agreement
- small size
- false modesty
- physics

- prayer
- smoke cloud

The girls are excellent judges of character and are thought to tailor their methods to the persons who they believe are seeking them. This, in any event, is what they have told us.

Around the age of fourteen or fifteen the girls lose their abilities. Some young women make fruitless efforts to retain them well into their twenties, but these efforts are regarded as socially unacceptable, and such young women are shunned. Outsiders assume that women should regain their abilities once they reach old age or otherwise lose their desirability, but this glib assumption is wrong, and evinces a fundamental misunderstanding of the girls' role in our community. Most find such logic offensive. Once the ability is lost, it cannot be regained. Women rumored to have relearned concealment are generally later found to have died or moved away.

Most women don't miss their juvenile powers. They don't remember how they did it. They don't care. Why should they?

It must be admitted that a very few women are thought to remain concealable for their entire lives. There are stories of ostensibly missing girls found dead in their homes decades later, as old women, the implication being that they were present all along, but unseen. Our museum features an exhibit of journals thought to have been written by such women. The entries read, "Watched them eat dinner," and "Bus didn't stop for me."

The journals, however, might be hoaxes. Most women think so. But the men want to believe.

Boys

The boys are expressing themselves through their bodies. They are making themselves known via a series of sudden motions, some fluid, most of them jerky, awkward, startling. They want you to react. The boys would like to be praised for the movements they have performed. To that end, they have composed sample comments and written them on three-by-five-inch note cards, in their execrable handwriting, and they pass these out to the girls and adults. Some of the cards read:

I am very impressed by your poking.

Your jumping out from behind that tree was excellent.

We love you very much. Thank you for convulsing in the grass.

Your spasms have improved my day.

Everything about your clapping is delightful.

The boys have something that they want to show you. They take you by the hand and lead you somewhere—an open field, a beach, a playground, a parking lot. When you reach the destination, there's nothing to see. The boys have become distracted, or wandered off. It is possible that they just wanted to relocate you. You were aware that this might happen, but of course you went anyway, the boys' enthusiasm is so infectious. You pretend to yourself that your new placement is actually kind of interesting. That the boys had it in mind all along that what you really needed was a change of scenery. Don't ask them if that's what they intended, though. They're onto other things now.

For instance, they are disrobing! The boys want to be naked. They laugh uproariously at one another's behinds and penises. You quietly encourage them to put their clothes back on, the pants at least, but instead they cover things with urine: a tree stump, some ants, a chain-link fence.

It's not clear whom these boys belong to. There are lots of adults around, but none claim ownership. The girls are off somewhere on their own. The boys make you uncomfortable—not just their nakedness. Their demeanor, indeed their very existence, seems to impugn your moral authority, your sense of self. You don't wish to meet the gazes of the other adults. You are ashamed.

But the boys—the boys are enraptured by their own corporeality. They are horribly alive.

Want (Cane)

In the park, I was sitting one bench down from an old man reading a neatly folded newspaper. A wooden cane, fashioned from a hardwood branch, sanded and lacquered, leaned against his knee. The man had the air of having done this exact thing every morning for decades. He didn't look up as people passed. He just read his paper and, occasionally, rested his free palm on the head of the cane and gently rocked it.

Then a long-haired kid came pounding by in old running sneakers and baggy jeans and snatched the cane away—just blew past like a gust and seized the cane with the greatest refinement and delicacy, and without the slightest adjustment to his stride. It took the old man a second or two to notice. A little flutter at the corner of his paper, and the cane was gone.

A couple of burly guys saw it happen and took off after the kid. I asked the old man if he was all right, but I didn't really care. I was jealous. Of the kid, I mean. I wanted the cane. I wanted to be able to steal a thing with such grace, to be young and an asshole again.

Want (Nut)

The kid—not my nephew, but my cousin's wife's brother's kid, whatever that makes him—reached across the Thanksgiving table and took a nut, I think it was a pecan, from the white china bowl. He had to sort of half stand up to do it, and nearly upset the gravy boat with his shirtsleeve in the process, but he managed in the end— grabbed the nut, sat back down, and readied himself to pop the thing into his mouth.

But Great-Uncle Luther said, "You really wanted that nut, didn't ya, kid? You're like a little squirrel over there, huh. You just had to have that goddamn nut."

The kid sat there with his mouth open, maybe trying to figure out how he should take this, or wondering whether he should eat the nut, or put it back, or what.

"If I tried to take a nut like that," Great-Uncle Luther said, "my old man would have beat me bloody. A nut was worth something in those days."

The kid shrugged and ate the nut. Later that night, in the kitchen, Great-Uncle Luther told my mother to get her fat ass out of the way and she punched him in the teeth.

Blue Light, Red Light

The boy was five. For some time—his whole life until recently—he had been an only child. But then there came a baby. The baby was a girl. The boy was initially inclined to dislike the baby, as upon its arrival it became the center of other people's attention, attention that had once been his alone. But as the months passed, he found himself increasingly compelled by the baby: its face, its small hands and feet. The way it was willing to stare at him for hours. Or what seemed like hours to the boy, for whom time was malleable and uncertain. And so, after long consideration, the boy grew to like the baby.

○

One evening soon after the baby arrived, when the boy couldn't get to sleep, he was permitted to stay up with the mother and the father and watch television. The parents nodded off, and a new show came on: a true-crime show. The boy watched it. On the show, a criminal had broken into a house and killed a family, including a baby, with a knife and a club. Neighbors, friends, and relatives told police that the family had recently experienced problems with a crazy man in their neighborhood. The crazy man was addicted to drugs and had intended to rob the family to buy more drugs. But instead of merely robbing them, he killed them. The police found the man hiding under a bridge in another town, surrounded by the family's possessions.

○

Among the images displayed on the true-crime show, over a sound-track of ominous music, were photos of the dead family members with their faces blurred, lying on their backs in pools of blood. The boy saw these photos. When the show was over, the boy went to bed. He didn't tell the mother and the father what he'd seen.

○

It seemed to the parents that the boy had forgotten the show. But he expressed worry about the baby. He asked the mother and the father if they locked the nursery door at night. No, of course not, they said. You should, the boy told them. Well, we can't, said the parents—we're always going in and out of there, in the dark. The boy didn't argue. One night he locked the nursery door from the inside, then pulled it closed, before he went to sleep. This made him feel better. When the baby cried in the night, the parents couldn't get into the nursery, and the boy heard a lot of shouting. The father eventually got the door open with a screwdriver. The boy was punished the next day: treats were withheld. He didn't lock the nursery door again.

○

He pondered the crazy man more and more. This was a real person—he had actually killed a baby. The police said they had caught him, but what if the man escaped? The boy lay awake at night. Sometimes he cried. He would get out of bed and go into the nursery to make sure the baby was still there. One night, it wasn't, and he screamed. But the mother had merely taken the baby out of its crib to feed it. The parents were angry at the boy again, and punished him again. But the boy didn't care about treats anymore.

○

The boy checked, surreptitiously, the locks on all the doors in the house before he went to bed each night. He disguised this behavior by explaining that he was looking for a lost toy, which he would then "find" in his bedroom. Soon he began locking doors during the daytime as well. When the boy remembered that the crazy man on the show had gained entry to the house by climbing through an unlocked window, he found the window lock mechanisms, and added those to his security routine. He wasn't tall enough to reach every window lock, but he had a plastic stool that he could carry from window to window, for the high ones.

o

It was hard to do all this without being detected. The father said, "Who in the hell keeps locking all these goddamn windows!" "Not me," the mother said. The boy also denied it.

"Well, it can't be Emily, can it," the father said. Emily being the name of the baby.

o

The boy overheard conversations between the parents that he understood were about him, and about his fixation on the door and window locks. He was taken to a doctor and asked why he performed this "locking behavior," but the boy did not want to tell anyone about the crazy man under the bridge. So he told the doctor that he was afraid of monsters. The doctor wanted to know what the monsters looked like, and the boy, thinking quickly, said that they looked like the father, except completely covered with hair.

The parents did not bring the boy back to the doctor after that.

o

Instead, the four of them—the mother, the father, the boy, and the baby—visited a department store at the mall, where the parents bought an object in a white cardboard box. In a photo printed on the side of the box, a baby slept peacefully in a crib while, in the foreground, a large, featureless globe emitted a calming blue light. At home, the father opened the box. The globe was inside. It was made of white plastic and rested on a small white plastic pedestal. But when you plugged it in and turned it on, it glowed blue.

o

The boy could read a little, and he knew from the box that this object was called Baby's Calming Globe.

o

But the boy was to learn that it had another function. That night the father sat on the floor of the baby's room with the boy. The boy wore his pajamas and the father smelled pleasantly of beer. The father said, "What this thing does is, it scans the house constantly, making sure everything is safe. It's blue now, see? That means the doors and windows are locked, and there are no monsters inside or outside. Blue means safe. If anything is wrong—and believe me, it's really sensitive, with top-of-the-line technology—it'll turn red. You got that? As long as this light is blue, everything is fine, and you don't have to check the windows and doors. We only have to worry if it turns red. Okay?"

o

The boy said okay. The father clapped the boy on the shoulder, then told him it was time for bed. When the boy's mother came in to say goodnight, she asked if he felt safer now, and the boy said that he did. Later, the boy heard the parents talking in low voices, and then he heard them laughing. And then everything was silent, and the boy lay alone, staring into the dark of his bedroom.

o

The boy had lied to the parents. He did not feel safe. In fact, as he understood the situation, the parents had just confirmed, with their purchase of Baby's Calming Globe, the existence of the very dangers that had frightened him. That the parents had alerted him to the true nature of the device indicated that they trusted him to help them protect the baby. And now, instead of staying awake to monitor the light, they had gone to sleep.

o

So the boy gathered up his blanket and pillow and stationed himself on the floor in the hallway outside the nursery. Blue light glowed through the crack under the door, and the boy could hear the baby turn over and babble in her sleep.

o

In the morning, the boy found himself back in bed, underneath the blanket, his head on the pillow. He leaped out of bed, alarmed. But his family were all fine—awake, and sitting at the breakfast table. They gazed at him with what looked to the boy like disappointment. They didn't mention the previous night's activities. The boy said nothing, just sat down and ate his cereal.

o

The next several nights were the same. The parents went to sleep. The boy reported for duty at the nursery door. Then, at some point, the boy woke up in his own bed. Clearly the parents were moving him there, perhaps when the mother rose to nurse. At times throughout each day, the boy would steal into the nursery to have a look at the light, to make sure it hadn't turned red. Sometimes, incredibly, it was switched off, and the boy would switch it back on.

o

After a few days, the parents got the message and left the light on all day.

o

The parents' unconcern was puzzling, even alarming, to the boy. They never seemed to monitor the light themselves, day or night. And when they expressed dismay, it was not at the danger they all faced but at the boy's preoccupation with the blue light. "Buddy, look at it," the father said, in evident frustration. "It's blue. It's always blue. That means we're safe." The boy nodded, as though he understood.

○

Were the parents stupid? Did they believe that the light itself protected them? The boy's fears deepened. The parents were incompetent.

○

Weeks passed. The boy's vigil continued, and the parents did less and less to dissuade him from continuing it. Indeed, they seemed resigned to it. Meanwhile, the boy began to wonder by what mechanism, exactly, the monitor light worked. How could the machine tell the difference between safety and danger? Perhaps it could distinguish a stranger from a family member—like the mother's phone, which worked only when she looked at it—or violent motion from ordinary movement. While the father was at work, and the mother had the baby in the kitchen, the boy performed experiments. He dressed up in his Darth Vader costume and presented himself to the light. He seized his stuffed Chewbacca and staged a mock fight. He could not trigger the red light.

○

Perhaps Baby's Calming Globe was more sophisticated than the boy had originally believed, and was capable of distinguishing pretend violence from real violence. But this seemed unlikely. The boy was growing concerned that his parents had been deceived. It would be necessary to test the device. To present it not with fake danger, but real danger, of a sort that the boy could control.

○

There wasn't much time. It was late summer, not long before school was to begin. The boy formed a plan. He waited until the mother had experienced a sleepless night, rising at all hours to tend to the baby. After a long morning of sitting in the neighbor's weed patch playing his handheld video game, the boy was served lunch. Then his mother said, "I'm going to feed your sister." She went into the living room, slumped on the sofa with the baby, and nursed it. Soon both of them were asleep, the mother sprawled face-up with her head thrown back and breasts exposed, and the baby sprawled face-down on the mother.

Their postures reminded the boy of the dead family from the true-crime show.

○

The boy hurried to his room and pulled out from under the bed a cardboard box of old newspapers and wood shavings that he had collected from the shed. From a kitchen drawer he retrieved the butane lighter his mother used to light the often-temperamental oven. He placed the flammable-items box on the nursery floor, checked to make sure that Baby's Calming Globe was switched on, and set fire to the shavings and newspaper.

○

The nursery filled with smoke. And now, to the boy's surprise, the flames leaped high into the air and licked at the lacy cloth that covered the baby's changing table. The lacy cloth caught with a gasp and was quickly consumed. The fire then moved to the curtains, which had been made by the mother from a fabric printed with bumblebees. And now the smoke began to pour out the door and into the hallway, and the flames began to darken the ceiling.

○

Baby's Calming Globe was still blue.

○

Everything happened fast, after this. The fire alarm in the hall emitted a shrill squeal. The mother appeared, holding her blouse closed with one hand and clutching the baby in the other. She screamed, ran down the hall, and returned with a fire extinguisher in place of the baby. But she couldn't seem to get it to work. She told the boy to get out of the house. He obeyed, running out into the yard, and the mother followed seconds later, holding the baby and shouting into her phone. The boy heard her shout at the fire department, and then at the father. The nursery window filled with fire: indeed, it looked as though the house were going to burn down. By the time the fire department arrived, the flames had consumed the nursery, the boy's room, and the parents' room. Firemen unrolled their hoses and aimed them at the fire; when the father arrived, it was all over. Half the house was black and smoking, and the corner of the roof was caved in.

○

Some time later, crouching in the yard in front of the boy, the father said, his teeth clenched, his face red, "Why? Why did you do this?" And the boy, understanding that he had done something very wrong, but still convinced that there was a larger issue at stake, the issue of the parents' deception at the hands of the unscrupulous department store, said, "It didn't turn red. I was watching, and it didn't."

○

Surely, the boy thought, the father would react with anger, or at least concern. Instead, he merely appeared confused.

"It didn't turn red," the boy repeated, "it didn't work." He knew that this was not the right thing to say, that it would not make anything better, but it was the only thing he had, so he kept on saying it, with increasing desperation and in between sobs, until the father loosened, at last, his angry grip on the boy's shoulders and took him into his arms.

Polydactyly

The child was born with polydactyly—that is, with an extra finger on each hand—and his parents disagreed upon the proper course of action, the mother believing the extra fingers should be surgically removed so as to make the child "normal," and the father insisting that the extra fingers, if preserved, would cause the child to become a piano prodigy. The father prevailed, and raised the child accordingly, exposing him daily to classical and jazz recordings, subjecting him to thrice-weekly lessons, and forcing him to attend countless concerts and recitals, where the child discovered that his enormous hands, which turned out not to have a single ounce of musical talent in them, were excellent instruments for loud clapping—a skill that the child, now an adult, still possesses, and employs ironically, and not without some bitterness over his misspent youth, every time he has the misfortune to visit his haggard, disappointed, and twice-divorced father. "Bravo, Father," he intones, bringing those six-fingered hands together whenever his father dares boast of an achievement, however inconsequential—walking to the drugstore, reading a newspaper article all the way to the end, moving his bowels. "Bra," the son says, clapping ever more slowly, so slowly that it's impossible to know if he's finished, "vo."

Marriage (Fault)

She says, What a mess.
>You can say that again, he says.
>She says, It's all my fault.
>No, it's okay, he says.
>It's not.

○

Later, he says, You know what. It was *my* fault. I'm sorry, he says.
>He hangs his head and leaves the room.
>Ten minutes later, she finds him. She's angry.
>What? he says.
>You, she says. You always take everything. Even the blame.

Marriage (Love)

She says, Do you love me?

He appears to consider the question.

Well? she says.

I'm thinking about it, he says.

She says, We're married! What the fuck is there to think about?

You're rather difficult, he says.

So what! So are you!

He appears surprised. I'm difficult? In what way?

Are you kidding? she says. Your passivity. Your stubbornness. The way you pretend that things are simple when they're not. Like right now. You're acting like I just asked you a simple question. You're sitting there trying to actually answer it!

But you're the one who wants it to be simple, he says. You just want me to say yes. I'm acknowledging the complexity of the issue.

She says, No, see, that's the simpleton's idea of complexity. It's actually not complexity, it's oversimplification. If you were smart, you would have answered the question as though complexity wasn't even a thing.

So, he says, when you say you love me, you're lying?

No, you moron. I do love you, but I'm privately acknowledging, to myself, that love is not simple. Then I am vaulting over that layer

of complexity and giving the rhetorically appropriate reply, because I
am a higher fucking mammal capable of complex fucking reasoning.

Hmm, he says.

Okay, she says, how about this. Do you think I'm fat?

No, he says.

All right then.

I mean, he says, you're fatter than when we—

No, no, no, she says.

But I like a woman who—

No! No. You haven't heard a thing I said.

I can only be myself, he says.

False, she says.

I don't see what other choices I have.

False.

I love you, he says.

I hate you, she says.

He strokes his chin for a little while. What layer is that? he says,
finally.

I'm not at liberty to say.

I was right about your being difficult, he says.

Saying that I am difficult is an insidious form of flattery to yourself, she says. By saying that I am difficult, you are saying that you
are man enough to handle me. When in fact you are a fucking pussy.

He says, By saying that you hate me, you are flattering yourself.
You are saying that you are woman enough to be married to someone you hate. Someone who is a fucking pussy.

Touché, she says, four days later.

Marriage (Game)

He is holding a hundred-dollar bill, folded in half. He says, I've written something on this bill. If you can guess what it is, I'll give the bill to you.

I don't want to play this game, she says.

Please.

We're married, she says. We share our money. The bill is already half mine.

Conceptually possessing fifty dollars is not the same thing as holding one hundred dollars in your hand, he says.

That's true, she admits. But I'm not going to play your game.

He says, Then you'll never know what I've written.

I don't want to know what you've written, she says.

Yes you do, he says.

He's right. She does want to know. But because he wants to show her, she says, No.

But then, five minutes later, she says, Fine. I'm not going to guess, but I want you to show it to me.

If you don't guess, you'll never get the money.

I don't care, she says.

So be it, he says, and unfolds the bill. In large black letters, he has written, YOU LOSE.

I hate you, she says, meaning it.

I'm sorry, he says, not meaning it. Here, he says. Take the money.

I don't want the money.

He gets up and walks out of the room, leaving the bill on the table.

When he returns, she is gone.

The bill, too, appears to be gone, until he looks more closely. A pile of ash lies in its place. Only one small corner remains, on which she has written, in a tiny, precise hand, SO DO YOU.

The Cottage on the Hill (I)

The first time Richard visited the cottage on the hill, he was in his early thirties and still married to Evelyn. Their children were small—the daughter six, the son three—and they still believed that their problems were temporary.

They learned of the existence of the cottage from a man in their town, a laborer whom they had hired to replace a rotting porch beam. The man told them that he had stayed in it himself, on a hunting trip, and that it was beautifully appointed and largely unknown even to those who lived nearby. That's because it was owned by the gas company, on land where it had a drilling claim, land not generally accessible to the casual hiker or hunter. But if you called the gas company—at the substation the cottage was near, not the main number—and asked to rent the cottage, they would offer you an attractive rate, and allow you to hunt on the surrounding land.

Richard and Evelyn did not hunt, but he found this strange arrangement enticing. Evidently there was a lake nearby, and the gas company provided wood for the woodstove (it was spring and still chilly at night) and a rowboat and fishing tackle. Perhaps a weekend getaway could be a balm for their troubles. Richard phoned the gas company substation and made a reservation, and a few weeks later the family drove the ninety minutes to the site, which was on a gravel road deep in the woods near a small dilapidated town.

The substation itself was a low cinder block structure enclosed by a chain-link fence, and when they pulled in at a mechanically operated gate, an attendant stopped them and asked, with some hostility, what business they had here.

"We're staying at the cottage," Richard said through the open car window.

The attendant, a stocky middle-aged man with an imposing brow and gruff manner, softened. He offered Richard a broad smile and an awkward handshake. "Oh, you'll love it, sir. My wife and I spent our honeymoon there. A lovely place." The man peered into the back of their car and winked at the children.

Richard and Evelyn enjoyed a laugh at the man's expense on the way up the hill from the substation. A honeymoon, here? But it was the first laugh they'd shared in some time, and they both felt that the vacation had gotten off to a fine start.

The hill, steep for the area, was grassy and treeless, save for a towering oak that stood at its summit. This oak, it turned out, sheltered the cottage, a compact, two-story building sided with yellow clapboard. Beyond the cottage, the hill sloped gently toward woods that bordered the lake.

While the children played in the grass, Richard and Evelyn went inside to unpack their things. The cottage interior was strange—darkly paneled, and divided into what seemed like too many small rooms. There were a tiny kitchen and sitting room on the first floor, along with a master bedroom barely larger than the bed it contained. A bureau was wedged into a small closet. Upstairs was the bathroom and, farther along a narrow hall, two more bedrooms, both even smaller than the one downstairs, each containing one small cot. Peculiar photographs hung in the hall, curled black-and-white images of heavily clothed people posed outdoors, staring blankly at the camera.

The construction of the house was such that, despite its small size, it never seemed to truly reveal its shape and dimensions; it would prove vexing, in the days to come, to find the door to the stairway, or to orient oneself upon exiting, even though nothing had changed and the layout could not have been simpler. The cottage also had an unusual, if not unpleasant, odor, a bit like roasting nuts or burned chocolate, the source of which could not be found. For all that, though, the place seemed adequate, and they chose to ignore its shortcomings and enjoy, as best they could, one another's company.

For the better part of a week, Richard and Evelyn and the children told stories around the fire, went fishing and boating, walked in the woods, cooked rustic meals, and sang along to songs played on Richard's guitar. As the days passed, employees came and went down below at the substation, and sometimes they caught sight of the family and waved. It was a funny little vacation, but it had, at least for a while, the intended effect—Evelyn and Richard regained some of their closeness, and they enjoyed their children more than ever before.

And yet what Richard kept returning to—lingering in the hallway on his way downstairs to join his family—were the old photos, unframed, each hanging from a single nail like a WANTED poster, so that they fluttered and swung in the slipstream of passersby. His mind had processed them as former vacationers, awkwardly posed at the woods' edge. But now he saw that their woods were different—sparse and coniferous—and the landscape surrounding them flat, barren, and almost alien, compared with this lush and hilly terrain. The subjects wore roughly tailored animal skins and heavy boots; their hats were tall and boxy, with mysterious slots and flaps. Some of them held weapons: rifles, mostly, but also machetes, and, in one case, an actual sword.

Who were these people? They seemed to stand in judgment of him. They gazed through him as though he were nothing but smoke. Out on the beach, watching the children splash and play at the water's edge, he felt the gentle breeze as a threat, a force that could blow them away.

Hidden behind the hill, the gas company substation thrummed like a hibernating animal. He held his wife's hand tightly.

Doors

In a basket hanging from the front porch eaves, which all winter has contained only a dead petunia, a robin has now nested and laid an egg, and the wife wants to avoid disturbing it. She asks the husband to try not to use the front door, and locks it to remind him. Instead, she says, he should use the side door, the one that leads through the mudroom and into the kitchen, whenever he wishes to enter or exit the house. In addition, there is a smell, the smell of mildew, emanating from the bathroom sink, and it bothers the wife, so she asks the husband to please keep the bathroom door closed, even when he isn't in there. He would like to honor her requests, and tries to, sort of. But he doesn't care about the bird and doesn't notice the smell, and as a result he forgets to use the side door to the house and to close the bathroom door behind him. And there is some unreasonable, hostile part of him that wishes to ignore her pleas about the doors entirely, as a protest against what he sees as her excessive sensitivities, her unreasonableness. And so, several times, he defies her deliberately.

To the wife, the house is a series of spaces that must be controlled, the borders between which must be monitored. For example, she is concerned, during the summer, about managing the temperature of rooms. She would like the day's heat to be kept out, and the night's cool to be kept in. She opens doors and windows at night and closes them in the late morning, when the temperature outside meets, then exceeds, the temperature inside. This regimen can, at times, be interrupted by sounds. If, for instance, a construction machine or chain saw is in operation outside, the doors and windows must be shut against it, even if it also means shutting out cool air. If, however, frogs are active in the pond down the road, she will open the doors and windows to hear them, even if it's hot out. Smells also may affect the pattern of open and closed doors. If part of the house smells musty, or of mice—or, as today, of mildew—that part of the house must be aired out, or shut off from other parts of the house. Cooking odors that are delicious before dinner, and should reach, ideally, into the far corners of the house, become bothersome after dinner, and should now be sealed away and dissipated.

The husband is annoyed by these machinations, even when he ostensibly benefits from them. For him, doors are an impediment. Walking through the house, in the throes of one project or another, he would like all doors to fly open before him so that he doesn't have to slow down while passing from room to room. His mind is on his goal, whether it is a box of nails or an apple or a book, and he can't keep track of which doors are supposed to be open and which are supposed to be closed. When the wife asks him, for the third or fourth time, to please leave a particular door open or closed, he is irritated both with himself for forgetting, and with her for caring. Ultimately he would like the status of doors not to be an issue in their marriage, and this desire sometimes takes the form of a rigid code of conduct that directly contradicts his best interests. If, for instance, they are enjoying an intimate moment together, and she gets up off the bed to close the door, he is annoyed, even though he doesn't want the children to walk in on them any more than she does. There is a part of him that would rather be hot all night, suffering, than bother with all the opening and closing of doors. There is a part of him that would rather just listen to the sound of a chain saw or road grader than close the door against it, and sometimes, when an unpleasant sound or smell or temperature intrudes upon their lives, he begins to get angry with her for her opening and closing of doors, even if she hasn't opened or closed them yet, even if she isn't home.

When the husband was a boy, his mother kept all doors to the outside closed at all times. She liked to be sequestered from the world. However, she preferred that interior doors remain open, particularly when her son was behind one. If he was in his bedroom, reading with the door closed, and she passed by, she would wordlessly open the door. If he locked the door, she would jiggle the knob and say, "Unlock this door." If he didn't unlock the door, she became angry. She often walked in on him when he was dressing or undressing. She went into his room when he was out playing or at school, and moved things around, cleaned them up. If things in his room looked like trash to her—notes written on scraps of paper, electronics parts, game pieces—she threw them away. He would come home to find his bedroom door open and his things moved or missing. The older he got, the more this angered him. When he finally moved out and went to college, he valued his privacy above all else, and hated the open, boundaryless nature of life in a dormitory. Friends learned to leave him alone, never to knock on his closed door.

But by the time he met his wife, he had changed. He had recognized, in himself, this reactionary trait, and had striven to eradicate it. In fact, he had overcompensated. Now he strode around the house naked, horrifying his children and surprising, on more than one occasion, some unsuspecting friend of his wife's who had stopped by for coffee. Now he played loud musical instruments or operated power tools without closing the door behind him, and filled the house with noise. Now he showered and used the toilet with the bathroom door open.

His anger at his wife for her careful control of the doors is, of course, anger at his controlling mother, even though his wife and mother are concerned with different types of control. But it is also anger at the former version of himself that allowed his mother to shape his personality.

For her part, the wife is well aware that her obsession with the opening and closing of doors mirrors a desire for other, less tangible kinds of containment and control. Her mind is a house full of doors that won't open and doors that won't stay shut. There are things she would like to do in her life that require access to certain areas of her mind, areas that, during childhood and early adulthood, were so easily accessed that they didn't even seem like separate spaces. Now they have turned out to be rooms with doors, and the doors are closed, locked, painted shut, and she cannot figure out how to open them again. Conversely, there are things that never worried her when she was younger, regions of anxiety she didn't realize existed, that have now taken control of her mind, and against which doors cannot be shut. She feels, at times, as though her mind has been ruined by adulthood. It is the children, in part, the existence of the children that has made her this way, and it is also the husband, with his inexhaustible impulses and desires, many of which involve her or demand her attention. But mostly she blames herself, and her susceptibility to these forces—the way she has allowed them to change her. As a young woman, it never occurred to her that this could happen to her mind. She is the same person, she is made of the same parts, but they have been reorganized. The sound of a chain saw outside, or the gradual heating of the interior of the house on a summer day, doesn't merely irritate her; rather, it inspires in her a feeling of panic, a sense that nothing can be contained or controlled at all. When she was a child, she would dream of finding secret rooms filled with mysterious and interesting objects: dreams of inspiration, of discovery. Now she dreams of rooms that fill with water, with fire—danger that enters through open doors, that cannot be expelled through doors that stay shut.

The husband is angry. Not at the wife, not yet, but at something else—a colleague, a failed project at work. He is angry and he wants to go out in the yard and stalk around with his hands in his pockets and his head down. But the front door is locked, because of the robin in the hanging basket. He is angry at what he's angry at, and now he is angry at the wife as well, for caring about the robin, and he is angry at the robin, and at himself for getting angry at the robin, the wife, and the thing he's angry at. He shouts an oath, unlocks the front door and flings it open, stomps across the porch and down the steps. Out of the corner of his eye he sees the startled robin fly away.

The wife, inside, in another room with the door closed, doesn't hear the husband. But she is thinking about the robin, wondering why she cares about the robin or its egg. It's just a bird, after all; there are plenty more where this one came from, and the others, the ones whose nests she can't see, are the smart ones, laying their eggs far away from human habitation. Indeed, perhaps this is the same damned robin that flung itself against the closed living room window just a few weeks ago, defending its poorly chosen home against its own reflection. The wife is trying to make herself·not care about the robin, to stop worrying about the children, to stop being bothered by the husband. In her mind, doors are flying open and slamming closed.

The robin, for whom there are no doors, whose mind cannot conceive of, nor would have any reason to conceive of, such a thing, perches high in a tree overlooking the house, wanting the egg: she wants to fly to it, settle on it, warm it. She wants to feel it beneath her. But there is a part of her that already knows it's too late. The nesting spot was no good. She has been frightened away from it too many times; the chick inside the egg is dead. The robin experiences her separation from the dead egg as a hollowness, a pain, in her breast. But already that pain is fading, her desire to return to the nest is fading, her fear of the man pacing in circles in the yard and the woman who opens and closes doors is fading. Everything below her, in fact, is fading, everything that is not the sky and the branch she feels, reassuringly, and with some small inalienable joy, beneath the claws that were made to do this precise and important thing.

TWO

As Usual, Only the Crows

In this town, there are people who like deer and people who dislike deer. The people who like deer dislike the people who dislike deer, and the people who dislike deer also dislike the people who like deer. For reasons of safety, people can't shoot deer for sport inside the town limits. So the deer dislikers would like the town to kill the deer, and the deer likers would like the town to protect the deer. Because everyone either dislikes or likes deer, the town cannot take a position on deer without alienating one group or the other. For this reason, the town has not taken a position on deer.

One group very much likes deer, but also would like the deer to be dead, and that is the crows. They would like as many deer as possible to live in this town, so that as many deer as possible will die in this town. The crows don't care what the town thinks about deer. They don't recognize that there is a town, or that there are people who like or dislike deer, or one another. The crows are more interested in dead deer than in live people.

As usual, all human beings involved in the situation are destined to remain dissatisfied. As usual, only the crows will get what they want.

Pins

All day the child has been trying to get the window open. He's four and he isn't strong enough. The father has noticed this, but it's winter, and he doesn't want the window open, so he's been ignoring the child's efforts. Eventually the child cries and the father asks him what's wrong.

"I can't open the window."

"Well, I don't want you to open the window. It's cold."

"But I have to get the pins!"

"What pins?"

"The *pins*."

What the child is talking about is a cache of small safety pins he slipped under the sash one unseasonably warm day when the window was open. He wants the pins because tomorrow he's going to preschool, and his friend Julia wears the same kind of socks he does, and he figures he can put the safety pins on his socks, so that they won't get mixed up. But today, anyway, this is beyond his power to explain.

The father goes to the window and looks out, into the yard. "I don't know what you're talking about."

Later that day the child manages to slide a metal ruler underneath the sash and is able to pry open the window. He sees the pins and reaches for them, but the ruler slips and the window crushes his hand. He wails in pain.

The father examines the hand. "I told you not to play at the window," he says. "I need the pins!" says the child. "Arthur, I don't know what you mean." "The pins! The pins!" "Please stop crying and tell me what you mean." "I *need* the *pins*!" The father is exasperated. The child is sent to bed early.

The next day, at school, the children make a puppet theater. They use their socks as puppets. The child's socks are mixed up with his friend's, and he returns home with a mismatched set. "This isn't your sock," his father says.

"I know."

"Where's your sock?"

"Julia has it."

"Then whose is this?"

"Julia's."

"Oh." The father scratches his head. "We should put your initials on them or something. Your socks. So you know they're yours." The father looks at the child's hand. It is discolored where the window landed on it. "Does this hurt?"

"No."

"What do you think? Should we put your initials on your socks?"

"Okay."

But they don't get around to it. The father is pretty busy and the child's mind wanders. Eventually the child is given new socks that look nothing like Julia's. Spring comes and the father replaces the storm windows with screens. He finds the little pile of safety pins. He says to himself, "Where the hell did these come from?" and throws them into a drawer.

Lost and Gone

There is a book in the house. She knows where it is and what it looks like. She wants it, so she goes to get it.

But the book isn't there, nor is there a gap in the row of books it might once have filled. The book has not been misplaced on its proper shelf, nor on the shelf above or the one below.

The book is a paperback with a brick red spine, black lettering outlined in white, and a black-and-white publisher's logo. This book is beloved, so the spine is cracked, and the corners bumped and furred.

She embarks upon a thorough search of the house. There are fourteen bookcases distributed across five rooms, so it takes a while. When the search proves fruitless, she performs it a second time.

She texts various friends, asking if she lent them the book. She doesn't even want to read it, really. She just wants to check a line she remembers, to make sure she has it right.

The friends don't have it. Her husband didn't move it to his office. It isn't in her car or her knitting bag or her old satchel, the one she retired because of the mouse smell.

It's only when she goes online to buy a new copy that she realizes she misremembered the book's appearance. It's ochre and green, with white lettering, and she finds her copy in its proper place on the shelf, the first place she looked. It's in much better shape than she had recalled.

She buys the extra copy anyway, and when it arrives, she squeezes it onto the shelf next to the old one. Now she has two of them.

But the one she lost is still gone. It's gone because it isn't real.

She got the quote wrong, too.

Fastidious

The fastidious man cleans his apartment before he leaves on a trip. He cleans it far more thoroughly than he does during his routine twice-weekly cleanings; one could say, then, that he values his absence more than his presence. He returns from his trip anticipating pleasure at entering his thoroughly cleaned apartment, but always feels disappointment, because now the apartment is occupied, by him. One could say, then, that the fastidious man regards himself as inherently corrupt.

SuperAmerica

At one time, the gas station on the corner, by the bridge, was called SuperAmerica. But by the time we moved here, it had assumed another name.

Our new friends, however, having lived here before us, still called the gas station SuperAmerica. And because they disapproved of our efforts to use the new name, we, too, began to call it SuperAmerica.

Since then, new people have moved to town, and have tried to use the gas station's new name, the one on the sign. Our disapproval has driven them to adopt SuperAmerica, as well.

At first, we were uncomfortable wielding this authority. We'd never legitimately patronized SuperAmerica, so what gave us the right to compel others to call it that?

Then it occurred to us that our friends, the ones who lived here before us, might also never have visited the true SuperAmerica.

It could be that many generations of residents had passed without firsthand knowledge of SuperAmerica. It could be that the gas station was called SuperAmerica only many decades ago, deep in the collective municipal memory.

It could be that it never was.

with apologies to Anne Panning

West to East

She is walking over the bridge between the north and south ends of town. Beneath her the creek rages and roils with spring runoff. She thinks, Isn't this creek supposed to flow west to east? The creek is flowing east to west. She remembers it distinctly—west to east. What distant cataclysm could have caused this change? She stops walking as an unspecific terror takes hold of her, and she grabs the guardrail. Then a woman brushes by with a child on a leash and says, "Don't bother the lady, Tractor." Tractor? Is that what the woman said? The child meets her eyes. That child is named Tractor! When she turns, at last, back to the creek, flowing east to west, she thinks, No, I must have remembered it wrong.

Marriage (Pie)

She says, What are you doing?

She has just walked into the kitchen. He is concentrating on something at the counter. It is clear by his posture that it isn't going well. He says, Nothing.

You are not doing nothing, she says. You've got a bowl and some flour there. And butter. You've got a bunch of fruit. I see a cookbook. You're cooking, she summarizes.

No, I'm not.

You are cooking, she says. Then she adds, You don't cook.

His shoulders twitch. He turns to look at the cookbook, revealing his face. It is tight and flushed.

He says, I am *baking*.

You don't bake, she says.

Well, it looks like you're wrong, he says.

She sits at the table. She takes out her phone and uses it to ignore him. Every few minutes, he emits a quiet oath. She laughs at something on her phone.

Look! she says. She holds up the phone.

He turns. His forehead is dripping with sweat. He wipes it away with his shirtsleeve, which is also sweaty.

On the phone's screen, an animal is doing something funny.

That's funny, he says, unsmiling, and returns to his work.

So, she says, putting the phone away. Why the fuck are you baking?

For fun, he says.

You're not having fun, she says. You're miserable.

So what if I am, he says.

If you suck at it, and it's not fun, what's the point?

He mutters a reply, too quiet to hear.

What? she says. Speak up.

I said, I was *reading* an *article* about *marriage*.

What does that have to do with anything? Marriage? What?

He grunts. A little cloud of flour rises up from the counter. He says, The article says you can make your husband happy by baking him a pie. So I'm baking you a pie.

You're the husband, you asshole, she says. I'm the wife.

Whatever, he says. The principle is the same. You're unhappy, so I'm baking a pie.

I'm not fucking unhappy, she says. Who said I was?

He doesn't answer. After a while she returns to chuckling at her phone. When, some time later, the sound of quiet sobbing reaches her from the counter, she puts the phone away and goes to him.

She says, You're doing it wrong.

No, I'm not.

Yes you are.

I've got the butter and the flour. And the sugar. And I'm putting them together and it's just a . . . it's crap. It's a ball of fucking crap.

Move.

No.

Don't be a baby, she says. Move over.

He steps aside, but not quite far enough. She pushes him with her hip. He stumbles with an exaggerated motion.

This butter is warm, she says. You need cold butter. And ice water. Where's the fucking ice water?

Ice water? he says.

For fuck's sake, she says.

She throws away everything he has done. Then she spends forty minutes clanking around in the kitchen, making a pie. She makes a crust and then she makes the filling and then she puts more crust on top of the filling and she puts the pie into the oven. During this time he retreats to the table and sits very still, with his head on his crossed arms.

When she joins him at the table, clapping the excess flour from her hands, he abruptly gets up, his chair clattering to the floor behind him. He runs from the room. A moment later, a distant door slams.

When the pie is ready, she takes it out of the oven, cuts a slice, and puts it on a plate. She brings it up to the bedroom. But the door is locked.

Open the fucking door, she says.

No.

I brought your pie.

I don't like pie, he says, his voice muffled by what sounds like a pillow.

Of course you do, she says. Everybody likes pie.

I don't like hot fruit.

You don't like *what*? What kind of fucking phobia is that?

I didn't say I was *afraid* of it, he says, more clearly now. I said I didn't *like* it.

Baking makes the husband happy, she says. I'm setting it down here in the hallway, and you better fucking eat it. I spent a fucking hour baking it for the sake of our marriage. You're going to grow up and eat it and it's going to make you happy. If I come up here in fifteen minutes and I don't see an empty plate outside this door, I'm going to break in there and fucking force-feed you marriage therapy. Do you understand?

He doesn't answer. She goes downstairs, serves herself a piece of pie, and laughs at funny animals on her phone while eating it.

Meanwhile, upstairs, the door opens a crack and a hand snakes out. It drags the plate of pie through the opening. The door closes.

A few minutes later, the sounds of crying can be heard, followed by the sounds of eating.

Marriage (Umbrella)

He says, It's raining. It wasn't supposed to rain.

What do you mean, she says, *supposed to*. There's no *supposed to* in weather. Weather just happens.

There's a picture of the sun on my phone, he says. There's suns all week. The TV said sun and the radio said sun.

She says, The weather doesn't care what your phone thinks.

Still, he says, I feel betrayed. I was told one thing and another thing happened. I have the right to be angry.

Well, she says, what were you going to do in the sun?

Walk downtown, he says.

She says, Why don't you use an umbrella. Remember your search for the perfect umbrella? You went through half a dozen. Fuck this fucking umbrella! you said, and you threw them all away. Except for the last one. You'd found it, you said. At last you could walk downtown in the rain. Where's that umbrella?

In the closet, he says.

So use that.

It turns out, he says, that I don't like walking downtown in the rain, even with the perfect umbrella. My feet and ankles get wet.

So who's betrayed now? she says. Your fucking umbrella, that's who. The umbrella's the real victim here. How would you like to be declared perfect then abandoned forever in a closet?

He doesn't answer. Twenty minutes later, she says, Hey! Hello? Where are you?

I'm in the closet, he says from the closet.

She says, What the hell are you doing in there? Have you been in there the whole time? What is wrong with you?

I came in here to look for the umbrella, he says, and I decided to stay.

Why? What on earth are you doing?

It's quiet. It smells like coats.

Jesus, she says. You've finally lost it.

You should come in here, he says.

Yeah, no, I don't think so.

But then, a few minutes later, she goes into the closet and shuts the door behind her.

See? he says.

Yeah, she says. I guess so. Hey, what the hell is that?

It's the umbrella, he says.

Oh, no, it's not, she says. That's your dick.

He doesn't reply.

I guess you want to have sex in here. That's what you've been doing, thinking about sex.

Among other things.

Well, maybe later. Right now I want to go downtown.

Have fun, he says, getting wet ankles and feet.

Actually, she says, the rain stopped. It's sunny now.

Suddenly his phone illuminates the closet. Look at that, he says. You're right.

So are you coming?

Sure, he says.

They bring the umbrella.

Marriage (Points)

He sends her a text message while they are both at work. A few minutes later, his phone rings.

Are you mad at me? she says.

No, he says. In fact, I just texted you.

I know, she says. You sounded mad.

He says, The text said, See you in an hour.

You didn't use any exclamation points.

It's a text. You don't punctuate a text.

Mitch does, she says. He ends his texts with exclamation points.

So go be married to Mitch.

Maybe I will.

Jesus, he says, are we done here?

I don't know, she says. You tell me.

They hang up. They don't meet for lunch, as planned. But in the
days that follow, he adds exclamation points to his texts. She doesn't
thank him, but she doesn't get mad, either.

He gets accustomed to the exclamation points. His texts to other
people start to seem rude to him, so he adds the points to those too.
One woman at his office begins texting him back more frequently
and enthusiastically. They joke and flirt at the photocopier.

One night, at home, a knock comes on the door. He answers. A man is standing there—a big man with a crew cut and a beer belly. Are you fucking my wife? the big man says.

Who the hell are you?

The big man takes a phone out of his pocket and holds it up. On the screen are the coworker's exclamation-point-laden texts.

Oh, her, he says to the big man. No. Did she say I was?

The big man says, When I asked her, she said, Wouldn't you like to know?

Whoa. No. No, I'm not.

What's with the texts, bro? the big man says.

They're just texts!

His wife approaches the door. She says, Are you fucking this guy's wife?

No! he says.

She looks at the big man's phone. You're sending some bitch exclamation points! Fuck you! Those are mine!

Hey now, says the big man.

I got used to them! he tells her. I started sending them to everybody!

Only I get the exclamation points! she shouts. They're mine! Other women get nothing!

Okay, okay!

The big man appears uncomfortable. He pockets the phone. Sorry to bother you folks, he says.

So you believe me? he asks the big man.

Oh yeah. Yeah, the big man says, backing away from the door. No worries, she's always been a psychotic lying bitch.

Later, in bed, he says, What kind of fucked-up marriage is that? and she says, Right?

The Loop

Divorced, fired from adjunct teaching after a botched attempt to unionize, and her only child lost to college, Bev had, for the first time in decades, more freedom than she knew what to do with. The empty house, hers alone, disgusted her: she sold it, against her daughter's wishes, and moved to a two-bedroom apartment in a new building downtown. Between the house money and the monthly support payments from her ex—he was fucking his assistant and had signed the papers with the heedless joy of a rabbit sprung from a trap—she'd been given the opportunity to think carefully about what to do with the rest of her life. This quickly came to seem like torture. So she volunteered for Movin' On Up.

This was the charity she'd donated her ex-husband's study desk to—a nonprofit whose volunteers drove a big yellow truck around town, collecting the castoffs of the well-to-do and delivering them to people in need. After her move, having settled into her newly purpose-less life, she realized that she actually missed moving—she was good at it, enjoyed the physical effort, the strategic tetrising of bureaus and bookshelves and chairs and lamps, the packing and unpacking. She recalled the energetic good cheer of the Movin' On Up crew, understood that she envied them, and gave the organization a call. Turned out they needed a driver. Could she do it?

Yes, she could. She reported for duty in the parking lot of a storage facility behind a strip mall on the edge of town, where the Movers (as they called themselves) stored mattresses, bed frames, sofas, and dining tables in donated lockers the size of rest-stop bathroom stalls. She was assigned a couple of big, strong kids—student athletes from the high school, looking for something besides football to put on their college applications—and was given a clipboard of addresses to visit. Every other Saturday she drove a rotating duo around town, and supervised them as they hauled heavy objects out of the basements and attics of the rich and up narrow staircases into the third-floor walk-ups of the poor. The donors were generally cheerful, embracing the opportunity to feel magnanimous while being relieved, by strangers, of a burdensome chore. They occasionally tried to tip the teens, who had been trained to refuse but probably did not when Bev was out of sight.

The recipients of the donated furniture were sometimes angry or paranoid, in the throes of mental illness or methamphetamine addiction. But most of them were delighted. They were people in transition, often fresh out of unemployment or the hospital or rehab, with just enough money to rent a cheap place to live and not a penny more to furnish it. The deliveries made them feel as though they were that much closer to having their shit together. Almost all of them were women.

The only time Bev felt that she had her own shit together was every other Saturday. The rest of the time she spent catching up on the recreational reading she'd failed to do for the past twenty years and idly perusing the websites of various professional and technical schools—welding, computer science, nursing. She took long walks with her sweatshirt hood up and her hands deep in her pockets, listening to political podcasts and trying to gin up the fury that she used to be capable of, and which had made her feel so alive. But the ex-husband had ruined it—she was tired even of rage. She took a cooking class and bought a video game console. She called her daughter every day, and felt lucky when the girl picked up. She counted the days until Saturday.

o

This Saturday began as they all did. She drove her car to Kim's house to collect the truck keys. Kim was the administrator; she spent her working hours padding around her living room in wool socks, arranging pickups and drop-offs with her phone in one hand and a placid toy poodle cradled in the crook of the other arm. As always, Bev idled her car at the curb, jogged up the porch steps, accepted the keys through the half-opened door, and saluted her farewell. Back in the car, she executed a slow U-turn in the cul-de-sac at the end of Kim's street.

It would not have occurred to her to remember this experience, the deliberate and careful arc around this bulb of pavement, but it was something she would later be forced to give a lot of thought to. The cul-de-sac was separated from a busy county highway by a chain-link fence and a drainage ditch; highway traffic massed there behind a red light—on this day, a garbage truck, an old brown sedan, a pickup flying a tattered Confederate flag. To the right stood a porta-john, attendant to a nearby construction site: Kim's neighbor was erecting a barn that Bev suspected would actually serve as a stealth rental cottage. Between the two houses, traffic cones were scattered, one lying on its side; behind them, a pile of muddy gravel had assumed a Vesuvian shape. On the left, the brutalist concrete walls of the university's ag school cooperative extension shone dully in the diffuse sunshine; somebody in a Buffalo Bills jacket was carrying a ragged-looking buff-colored hen through its door. An SUV was parked out front; it probably belonged to the chicken's keeper. The cul-de-sac was cracked and pitted, and filthy water pooled in the potholes. The wheels of Bev's car communicated the pavement's every flaw. She considered having the suspension checked.

At the storage lockers, Bev was to meet this week's Movers, a boy and a girl. But the boy was a no-show. Bev had his cell number on her clipboard; she texted him and then, a few minutes later, called. Someone answered with a groan and immediately hung up.

She and the girl stood, blinking at each other in the autumn air. Did they have the muscle to go it alone? "Wiry" is what Bev's ex-husband had once called her, pushing her unfinished bowl of ice cream closer. The girl, Emily, looked half-asleep, resentful, so it surprised Bev when she agreed to work without the hungover defensive lineman.

"You sure?" Bev said. "There's two loveseats, some beds. A bookcase."

"I need this," the girl replied. "For my A in Government."

"Keep your back straight, use your hips and knees."

Emily nodded.

"All right. Let's go."

Movin' On Up liked to minimize the amount of furniture kept in storage—the lockers were infested with bugs and mice and flooded easily—so Kim had scheduled this morning's donations to be distributed in the afternoon, along with a few items already packed into the truck. First stop was at the northern edge of town, up on the lake: a greened and groomed strip of mini-mansions, each paired with a matching boathouse and dock. Small yachts bobbed on the wind-raised chop. A woman was donating a loveseat and an end table. "Thank God," she said, "the new sofa will be here any minute," as though she were irritated at them for being late, which they were not. The loveseat was discolored and shredded; its odor implicated a cat. The rules forbade pet dander but everyone ignored them.

Bev and Emily grunted their way up the truck's narrow ramp, taking frequent breaks, and shoved the loveseat against the truck's wall. On the way back to the county two-lane, they passed the van delivering the new furniture; the driver honked at them, annoyed at having to pull over on the access road to let them by.

Next up, a king-size mattress in an affluent suburb. A note on the spreadsheet read, "Do not knock. Take from garage. Door code is 3912." Low-hanging maple boughs scraped the truck as Bev backed down the driveway; a man in a necktie—on Saturday!—scowled at them through a bay window. The mattress was rolled up, held fast by bungee cords and stained by the oil that saturated the garage floor. As they flopped it into the truck, the man came out to reclaim, indignantly, his bungees.

A friendly old guy working on a motorcycle across from the public library helped them hoist his coffee table into the double-parked truck as peeved motorists honked and roared past. A trio of graduate students surrendered a sagging bookcase from their creekside rental with obvious relief. Just half a block away, Bev knew, her ex and the assistant shared a charming renovated carriage house, behind a towering Victorian owned by some university dean or other. She hated herself for occasionally strolling by, as though inadvertently. The cottage was shaded by a huge and ancient sycamore tree; a chrome orb, perched upon a wrought iron stand, stood in a neatly maintained rock-and-moss garden. Was the orb the assistant's? Did she subscribe to new age principles and styles? From where they were dragging the grad students' bookcase, Bev could see the assistant's sporty red coupe, parked obediently at the curb.

○

Bev was relieved to move on to the next donor, a jolly downtown lady with a queen-size mattress, box spring, and frame; a tired-looking teenage boy, surrounded by books and papers, glanced up from the sofa as they inched the bed down the hall. Seeing the boy, Bev experienced a jolt of sorrow. She wanted to bring him a cup of tea or a slice of buttered toast, even if the toast went uneaten and the tea grew cold.

"Maybe you know my daughter," Bev said to Emily on the way to their last pickup. "Celeste."

The girl narrowed her eyes, whether in confusion or vexation, Bev couldn't tell. The two couldn't be more than a year or two apart in age.

"Celeste Dreyer?" Bev prompted.

"Ohh," came the reply. "I know of her."

Bev had been flirting with the notion that this girl reminded her of Celeste—or, rather, of Rose, which was the name, announced via text message, that her daughter had for some reason chosen to be addressed by from now on. There was something in the guardedness of the eyes, the determined set of the shoulders. But Bev's daughter was more prone to assert herself with her body than this girl was—Celeste had a fleshier body than Bev had ever had, inherited from her bearish father, and quite like the assistant's, Bev hadn't failed to notice—and was more reactive to the world around her. Celeste was a twitchy girl, easily upset, but also sharp-witted when she wasn't angry, and quick to laugh. No, it would come to her, who it was that Emily reminded her of, but now it was time to get out of the truck and accept the final bed frame.

This one would be trickier, though. The donor was a housebound woman, confined to a kind of mechanical cart; she was curled in on herself like a leaf in winter and her hands clutched the air. Accompanying her was a hired aide who was also caring for a round-headed six-month-old boy. The apartment, a one-bedroom in a subsidized complex out by the college, was cluttered with baby things—an enormous stroller, a playpen and a crib, a huge package of diapers. Empty baby-food jars and formula bottles filled the sink. The aide's English was poor, and she used it to argue with the donor about which items she wanted to donate.

"No, no, you say the spring box."

"No, Greta, I mean the frame, the metal frame."

"Is no frame, only box."

"No, there's no box, just a metal frame, underneath the mattress."

It soon became clear that the donor hadn't been in the bedroom for some time; the cart prevented it. A hospital bed had been set up in the living room, among the child's things. The donor was giving away her old bed, the bed of her healthier days.

"It's only the frame you want to donate?" Bev asked.

"I'm keeping the mattress—my son wants the mattress," the woman said, her speech effortful but clear. Bev wondered what the son thought of this arrangement—the aide and her child taking over the apartment, his mother an afterthought. She wondered what the donor thought of her son, tolerating this.

The debate continued, pointlessly, for another minute, until Emily, who had stood in stunned silence since they entered, pulled her phone from her pocket. "Why don't I take a photo?" she said. "You can look at it and tell us what you want us to take." They waited in silence as Emily disappeared into the hall; they saw the flash and heard the synthetic shutter sound of the phone camera. The picture revealed that both women were right: the son's future mattress rested on a box spring crookedly overhanging a low metal frame, its casters sinking into the pile carpet. "So you want us to take both things?" Bev asked. "The box spring and the frame?"

"Yes. Yes."

"And leave the mattress behind for your son."

"That's right."

She and Emily got to work in the bedroom, leaning the mattress up against the window and hauling the box spring to an upright position. They were trying to figure out the proper handholds when Bev happened to glance down at the floor.

"Wait," she said. "Where's the frame?"

"What?"

"The metal bed frame. Did you move it somewhere?"

The carpet was empty of all but a few dead insects, some dust bunnies, and four depressions, the size and shape of cigarette lighters, that the frame's casters had left.

Emily squinted at the floor, then at the bottom of the box spring, as though perhaps the bed frame had stuck to it. "I don't get it," she said.

"Is this the same room?"

"It's the only one."

They stared at each other. Then Emily took her phone out of her pocket and looked at the screen. "It was right here," she said.

"Is it . . . in the closet?" Bev asked, though the sliding closet door exposed a packed wall of junk into which even a pillowcase would have been hard to wedge.

The girl scowled. "No!"

"Okay, okay. Well. I guess . . . we just take the box spring?"

But Emily did not want to let it go. "Where's the frame," she said.

"Is it . . . are you sure you showed them the right picture?"

"I only took the one!" She sounded as though she might cry.

"I mean, was there a different picture, already on—"

"No, Mrs. Dreyer, no. No! That was the picture I took!"

"All right."

"It was here!"

They stared at each other, realizing simultaneously that the other women had been listening to them argue. The baby cooed and the aide shushed him. Wordlessly, they lifted the box spring and stutter-stepped it into the living room.

"It looks like there isn't a frame, after all," Bev said. "So we'll just take the box spring."

The donor's face was blank. The aide frowned, eyes narrowed, as though worried she was being tricked, though it was unclear what the trick might have been. As Bev watched, her expression softened into quiet triumph—she was right, after all, that there was no bed frame, only a box spring.

Bev handed the donor a receipt and they dragged the box spring out to the truck. It was time to give it all away.

○

Silence, as usual, presided over the ride to the first client's apartment, though a different silence from before. Emily, head hanging and foot twitching, seemed angry; a couple of times, she pulled out her phone and stared at the photo of the missing bed frame, before putting it away with a sigh. As for Bev, she was accustomed to, and adept at, having to negotiate unexpected fissures in her life, and she had a knack for smoothing them over, making her world appear to have healed. Stability—that was what Bev had provided Celeste when her father moved out, during her junior year of high school, an ostensibly vulnerable time in any teenager's life. Which is why it bewildered her when the girl had seemed not merely to weather the rupture but to enjoy the novelty of it, to use it as a springboard to independence. Last summer, in the weeks before Celeste left for college, she would utter the assistant's name in Bev's presence with a casual, cruel insouciance that surely, surely she knew hurt her. Celeste would tell Bev that she'd gone to the pizzeria or the movies with her father and the assistant, that she'd taken a day trip to the city with her father and the assistant. As she talked, Celeste would jingle the thin silver bangles the assistant had bought her—a new, horrifying tic that it was apparently Bev's burden to ignore.

Why? Why?!

So Bev had it in her, here in the truck, to pretend that what had just happened hadn't: that the metal bed frame had not, in fact, mysteriously vanished from the woman's bedroom. Was Emily putting one over on her, maybe as some kind of retroactive, once-removed reprisal for something Celeste had said or done to her last year? But she knew it couldn't be so. The two hadn't known each other, and the girl was completely baffled.

The first client, a Black woman of around thirty, was clearly thrilled to see them; she lived in the subsidized apartment complex overlooking the hospital and had the air of somebody getting a fresh start—new job, new place. She needed the loveseat and the end table. She followed them out to the truck and helped them carry in the former. When Bev brought in the table, the woman put her hands on her hips and said, "Oh, oh. I'm sorry, I meant the other one. Can I get the other one?"

The table was a square of fake-wood-grain Formica with pitted chrome legs—not hideous, and sturdy enough. It was the one they'd picked up earlier that morning, from the woman who gave them the loveseat. Bev said, "I think this is the only one."

"No," the client said. "The little white one. The painted wood one."

The truck contained no such table. Bev was sure of it—she had literally just come from inside. But when she followed the client up the ramp, it was perched atop the mattress pile as though it had flown in and alighted there: a little white wooden drop leaf, just as the lady had said. It seemed impossible that it had remained upright as they drove; and, anyway, it had not been there moments ago, when they'd exhumed the loveseat from underneath the mattresses. Bev could feel Emily's body tensing beside her.

"That one!" the client reiterated, pointing. Dutifully, Bev climbed

back into the truck and gently carried the table down to her waiting arms.

o

After that, the run behaved better: nothing obviously inexplicable,
or even out of the ordinary, occurred. An old lady in public housing
whose grandson had broken her coffee table; a talkative Iraq War veteran living in a silver trailer in somebody's back yard on a grassy hill-
top, whose lumbar pain demanded a new mattress. A young couple
with twin babies and only one crib. A lesbian couple in a converted
hunting cabin who needed kitchen chairs. Later, Bev would have occasion to revisit these scenes, to try to figure out where the anomalies
lay—she knew they were there, knew that something was different.
She could feel the flaws in the day, much as, nearly twenty years earlier, she'd sensed that her water was about to break, ushering Celeste
into the confusing and hostile world. But the flaws remained hidden.
They couldn't all be for her—this world created chaos for its own reasons, unknowable ones.

And, as they drove and lifted and schlepped, Emily came to seem
more and more familiar to Bev, looked like somebody she used to
know: a nervous flick of the tongue, fingers worrying at a scar on her
knee. A fleeting glance from underneath the curtain of hair, which
ought to have been pulled back for work but wasn't, as though being
able to hide were more important than seeing what she was doing.
Bev wanted to ask, "Where do I know you from?" But the question
would have been ridiculous, as the memories were certainly from before the girl was born.

They arrived, at last, at their final stop, where they were supposed
to deliver a complete bed to a woman living alone in the development behind the Staples and the PetSmart. She would be getting
only a mattress and a box spring—the frame intended for her was
the one that had disappeared.

"I can't believe we're almost finished," Emily said, a rare un-
prompted remark, as they pulled up on the cracked and weedy asphalt apron that surrounded the apartment block.

The spreadsheet read, "Do not knock, call instead." Bev said, "You want to give her a ring?"

The girl unlocked her phone, then quickly dismissed the photos app, which still displayed the bed-frame picture. She keyed in the client's number, held the phone to her face, waited. Bev, meanwhile, turned off the engine, jumped down to the pavement, and heaved up the truck's rear door. No surprise: the bed lay alone on the floor, slightly askew, the mattress's corner hanging over the box spring's edge. She pulled out the metal ramp and greeted Emily as she came around the passenger side of the truck.

"No answer," she said. "It was like, 'This number is unavailable.'"

"Hmm." Bev peered at the woman's door, fortuitously on the building's ground floor: NO. 43. It was slightly ajar.

"Uh," Emily said.

"Let's see." Bev approached, taking note of a small face near the doorsill: an orange tabby, sniffing the air. The cat withdrew as Bev came near.

"Hello?" she called out, knocking. Her knuckles pushed the door open by another inch or two, and she was greeted by a gentle gust of air, extremely warm and dry, that carried the smell of cigarettes, wet cardboard, burned plastic, and ammonia.

The apartment appeared quite dark at first, and then, as Bev's eyes adjusted, clarified into dimness. She was standing in a small living room. Its one window had been covered by flattened cardboard boxes held together with masking tape; a single shadeless table lamp glowed in a corner. If the room contained any furniture, Bev couldn't see it. Household debris climbed in uneven piles toward the ceiling and walls: bulging trash bags, dirty clothes, plastic bins spilling children's toys, scratched and battered saucepans, cereal boxes, aluminum foil balls, baking trays, half-dismantled old televisions with shattered screens, plastic stereo equipment herniating skeins of wire, grilling utensils, and a dented hibachi bearing the logo of a hockey team. Cats—more than Bev could count—crept around the base of the junk mountain, and into and out of gaps between the items.

It was very hot in here. Bev heard a banging noise from around a corner—the slam of a skillet against a metal sink. Water was running.

"Hello?"

The banging stopped and then, after a moment, so did the running water. A cat darted out from the shelter of the hibachi into the harsh fluorescence emanating from the kitchen.

"Ma'am? We're here from Movin' On Up?"

The creature that stepped into the room was ghoulish, insectile: a woman of indeterminate age, malnourished, her single piece of clothing (a long T-shirt printed with cartoon characters) dangling from the wire hanger of her shoulder blades. And yet she moved with grace, as though she were even lighter than she appeared. Steam rose from the cast-iron skillet clutched, with maniacal intensity, in her right hand, and water dripped from it onto the floor, where a cat soon appeared to lick it up. She threw a glance over Bev's shoulder and shouted, "Don't let the cats out!"

It was Emily that the woman was shouting at; the girl stood frozen in the open doorway. Shocked into action, she slammed it shut.

The woman returned her attention to Bev. "What are you doing in my house."

"We brought your bed."

"Huh?"

"We're from Movin' On Up. You needed a bed?"

The woman's eyes clouded, then cleared. "Yes. Yes. You got the bed?"

"Out in the truck."

"All right. All right," the woman said. "Bring it in. Don't let the cats out."

○

Muscling the box spring to the door, Emily said, "I don't like this situation, Mrs. Dreyer."

"No, it's not great."

"I think this lady is on drugs. I think she needs help."

"I agree."

The client's bedroom lay around the corner; they would have to upend the box spring to get it through the kitchen, which was little more than a narrow hall with a stove and a sink at one end. The clutter continued here, towers of food containers and cat-litter tubs sharing the space with piles of laundry, empty bleach bottles, and, incongruously, a tall stack of cardboard jigsaw puzzles in boxes, the lower ones crushed, their pieces spilling out. Cat kibble crunched underfoot, and the oven was open, pushing blazing heat into the cramped space. Bev felt her sweat evaporating before it could even stain her clothes.

When they reached the bedroom, the reason for the client's need became clear: the entire far corner of the space had caught fire, and part of the futon still lying on the floor had been consumed. The carpet, walls, and ceiling were blackened; the many empty cigarette packages scattered around the space suggested a cause. A melted electrical-outlet cover still had a cord trailing from it, attached to the charred skeleton of a table lamp.

The ruined futon was covered in cats. Emily said, "Um."

"You gonna take this out of here?" the client asked.

"No, ma'am. We can't do that. Did you tell your landlord about what happened?"

The woman appeared to think the question over. "Yeah, he knows," she replied, unconvincingly.

"Okay."

"How do I get rid of this thing?"

"I'm not sure," Bev admitted.

They lifted up the futon, scattering the cats, and slumped it against the wall, blocking access to a tiny bathroom dominated by litter boxes. The clean area of carpet that was revealed looked bizarre: a rectangle of dark blue Berber empty of debris, save for a single scrap of pink paper. Bev picked it up: a movie ticket, from a superhero blockbuster she'd taken Celeste to see the week before she left for college. When Bev raised her head, the client was gazing at her expectantly. She couldn't toss the ticket back onto the floor; it would seem like an insult. And she couldn't keep it, because it wasn't hers. So she stood there, folding the ticket between her thumb and forefinger, for what felt like an eternity, until the client looked away. Bev shoved the ticket into the pocket of her jeans, and, with Emily, went out to the living room to collect the box spring.

It took longer than it should have. The thing could barely be wedged into the kitchenette; they had to move the puzzles and empty litter boxes, and even then they ended up scraping some paint off the corner of the wall. By the time they reached the bedroom, the futon had fallen back into its place on the floor.

Except it hadn't. It was still sagging against the wall. But it was also on the floor. There were, it appeared, now two of it. The client was smoking dispassionately, staring at the new one.

"What happened here?" Bev asked.

"Don't ask me," the client replied. "You moved it."

"There's another one?"

The woman just shook her head.

This new futon was identical to the last, sweat- and piss-stained, charred on one corner. The cats were nowhere to be seen—presumably they'd fled to the bathroom.

"Okay," Bev said. She could feel Emily bristling behind her like a guard dog. "Okay, well, let's just put it up against the other one."

They wrestled the second futon up against the first, pushing and kicking it to keep it in place. Then they fetched the box spring from the hall and let it thump into place.

Out at the truck, Emily said, "I'm not going back in there." Her arms were crossed over her narrow chest and she scowled at Bev. "I'll help you get the mattress to the door. That's it."

"Okay."

"This isn't what I signed up for. It's fucked up."

"You don't have to go in, Emily."

"Good, because I'm not."

It came to Bev, suddenly, who Emily reminded her of. Two years ago, Celeste's father had told her she could take a weekend trip, with a bunch of friends, to a mountain cabin that some boy's family owned.

He hadn't consulted Bev, because, apparently, he and Celeste had agreed that Bev would be unreasonable about it. Celeste admitted as much when an overheard phone call inadvertently revealed the plan. "You will not go!" Bev said, proving their point. She shouted it at her daughter in the hallway of their half-empty old house—a creaky Craftsman on the flats, expensive to heat and plagued by hidden decay. At the end of the hall, behind Celeste, hung an enormous ornate mirror that the previous owners hadn't bothered to unbolt from the wall when they left; it showed a reflection, partly obscured by the de-silvering glass, of her daughter's tense shoulders, and, deep in the shadows and very small, her own remote figure, arms crossed, as fiercely powerless as a cornered tomcat.

That's who Emily was like: herself, not Celeste. The lanky frame and coarse hair, the cluster of freckles over the long, humped nose. Now another image came to Bev, this time a photo her father had snapped at a high school track meet: young Beverly frozen in the act of passing the baton to her teammate. It was objectively a great picture, dramatic and flattering and perfectly framed, but Bev remembered the instant after it was taken, remembered letting go of the baton too soon, a half second before her teammate's hand would have closed around it, and the sound of it ringing dully on the asphalt. This was the photo that her father had framed, that he still kept on the mantel along with snapshots of Celeste throughout her life and—vexingly, as though the divorce had never happened—a family portrait from Bev's wedding day. "That's how I like to remember your mother," he explained, and that was that.

Bev and Emily carried the mattress to the door, and Bev dragged it through the apartment alone. She dropped it onto the box spring while the client stood, two cats cradled to her chest, watching with suspicion. "Are you going to be all right?" Bev asked as she backed out of the room, hazarding a final glance at the two identical burned futons, now collapsed into a mound on the floor. The client pretended not to understand the question.

The run was over. It was time to go home.

o

Emily said nothing during the drive back to the storage lockers. When they arrived, Bev signed her school form and thanked her for her help. "Sure," the girl said, turning to leave. She climbed into a dented sedan and carefully made her way off the lot and back to her life.

Bev locked the truck and walked to her car. It was evening. Curtains of rain obscured the hills in the distance, but here honeyed light illuminated the nearby veterinarian's office and the Turkish restaurant and the DMV. Gulls hopped and bobbed around a pile of French fries and their dropped paper basket, and a couple of kids made out in front of the defunct bowling alley. Bev's freedom and loneliness felt beautiful. She climbed in behind the wheel and headed for Kim's house.

On the way, she passed a little red coupe, its two inhabitants scowling, their mouths moving: an argument. It was, of course, her ex, being ferried about by the assistant, her white fingers gripping the wheel, her golden hair tugged and flattened by the air flowing through the open window. Bev ought to have felt a bitter satisfaction at glimpsing this moment of disharmony. "See?" she could say. "The new one's mad at you too." Instead, it reminded her of their fights about Celeste: his coddling of the girl, his enthusiastic embrace of her new name, of "Rose." She did all the work, he got all the glory! And a new woman to argue with, too.

Well, he could have it. Her ex's eyes met hers and he kept them there, his head turning as the two cars passed, as though it were some kind of surprise to him that she still existed, that she would continue to haunt him as long as they both lived in this dumb town. A minute later she arrived at Kim's. She turned over the keys and the clipboard, and ratted out the final client while scratching the poodle's head. Could the dog even walk? Bev had never seen it walk. Maybe it couldn't. Maybe this was Kim's cross to bear, to ferry her ailing dog from room to room for the rest of its life. Bev became aware that she was jealous of Kim. She was jealous of the poodle.

Later, she would wonder if it was the closing of Kim's front door that marked the beginning of it—the perhaps unintentionally heavy thunk of wood striking wood, the snick of the latch, the gentle clank of the pressed-tin WELCOME sign bouncing against the decorative cut-glass window. It felt appropriate, as a metaphor.

But eventually she would come to realize that it was the cul-de-sac where the shift took place. That slow circumnavigation past highway and ditch, the mountain of gravel and the porta-john. Somewhere in there, evening shaded back into morning, because the end of it was always the same, with the SUV and the Bills fan with the sick chicken. It was the light: that's how she could tell—the angle of the light changed, not in a flash but in a gradual sweep, like a bare bulb swinging at the end of a cord. By the time she'd gotten around the cul-de-sac, it was morning again, that same morning, and she was on her way to the storage lockers to meet Emily, and they were to begin their run, to do it all over again—the house on the lake, the king mattress in the garage, the motorcyclist, the grad students. The jolly mother with the quiet teenage son. And then the disabled woman and her aide, and the missing bed frame, the little white drop leaf table perched on the mattress stack. The old woman and the war veteran and the couples, and at last the tweaker with the cats and the charred bedroom, slowly filling up with identical futons like a bag of microwave popcorn. Then back to the lockers, and back to Kim's, the ex and the assistant, and back to the cul-de-sac to start again.

It was as if there were two Bevs: the one that experienced the day for the first time, and this one, the one she regarded as herself, trapped inside the other. She could read the mind of her original, could see what she saw, could feel the body inhabiting her actions. But she couldn't shout back, couldn't compel the first Bev to change a single thing: not a movement or a perception, not a word or a thought. The first dozen cycles, the first hundred, she screamed silently at First Bev to wait, just wait, let me think, let me see. But eventually she gave up on that. It was clearly one of the rules of whatever was happening: nothing could change. She could only observe.

So she convinced herself that observation was the way out. There was something she was supposed to notice, something the forces of this mad world wanted her to perceive before she would be freed to finish her life, to experience newness every second until death. That's what had been taken from her—the absolute pristine uniqueness of each boring moment of existence. For a long while (and who knew how much time was passing outside the loop—seconds? millennia?—or perhaps the universe was idling, just waiting for her to finish), she searched for whatever it was that she was supposed to find. Somewhere in the mundane chaos of that ordinary day, there had to be something: a detail she'd missed the first time, and then again and again and again. In the jolly woman's house, something written in the boy's notebook. In the silver trailer on the hill, the yellow meadow of sticky notes adhering to the fold-down breakfast table, what did they say? The faces in photographs in the grad students' rental. A voice on the radio from the motorcyclist's kitchen window. She would discover the existence of a single detail, then spend the next dozen cycles waiting for the moment when she could seize it, perceive it, fix it in the mind's eye. The day, she believed, was not infinite. If there was something to be seen, she would see it, and she'd be liberated, and relieved of the burden of this terrible, ancient memory.

At least that's how she felt in the beginning, or, rather, in what turned out to be the beginning: her enthusiasm for the task before her was motivated only by the promise of release. Then, gradually, she began to forget. First her memories of life before the loop faded, and were supplanted by memories of earlier cycles: particularly rewarding runs of observation and perception that resulted, initially, in extraordinary feats of deduction; and, later on, in the epiphany that it was not necessary to reach conclusions, only to observe and catalog; and, later still, in the acceptance of the superfluity even of memory itself. Her powerlessness had become a new kind of power, an infinity lodged inside the finite. She wondered, while it was still possible to care about such things, why she couldn't have performed this alchemy during her life before the loop, transforming her shortcomings as a mother, a mate, a teacher into this magisterial indifference.

Was this how gods were born? Had she become one? A time arrived when she knew that's what she was, a god, and with that knowledge came a contentment and a pleasure that she had never known in life. And eventually the knowledge faded, too. All that remained was the pleasure, disembodied and limitless, the loop itself nothing more than a decoration, like the pointless stars etched onto the bowl of the sky.

Cleaning (Dust)

That summer I worked as a custodian at my old elementary school. My supervisor was a deaf man in his early thirties called Vic. His speech was labored, but he could make himself understood, with effort. He didn't talk about his life, and I didn't ask. I just did the tasks he assigned me while playing my boombox as loudly as I wanted.

On breaks, Vic shared conspiracy theories. I don't know where one got these ideas in 1985. Magazines? He believed a lot of local people were Russian spies, and that Jews were stealing part of his paycheck. He thought that the dust that gathered in the corners of the school could give you AIDS. So he always assigned the task of sweeping to me. When he told me to sweep up the dust, he would point, and say, "Pick 'em up. Pick 'em up."

Years later, he ended his own life. In my mind, I connect his death to his conception of dust as *them*. If dust is plural, how many dust are there? A lot. You don't want to think too hard about how many tiny things there are, that you have to pick up. You just clean until things are clean, and *not a second longer*.

Cleaning (Off)

My first and only date with N ended when, after the delicious candle-lit dinner she had made, after the excellent conversation, the bottle of wine, and the smoky glances, I endeavored to wash, by hand, the dishes. I scrubbed each glass and plate with a soap-infused kitchen sponge, then rinsed it and placed it gently on the drying rack, and at some point in this process N touched my wrist and said to me, "Don't you think that's enough?"

"That what's enough?"

"The rinsing. Do you need to rinse each one so much?"

"I need to get the soap off."

"It's good enough," she said.

I continued to wash and rinse, placing each item into the rack the instant the last of the soap had been sluiced away.

"Stop," she said. "That's enough. I can't watch this." She took my hand and led me, not to the bed, but to the door. She handed me my coat.

"Thanks for coming over."

"I don't understand," I said.

"You didn't," she said, her mouth curdling in disgust, "have to get it *all off.*"

Jim's Eye

A bicyclist gives me the finger as I drive past him on the road, and for some reason this reminds me of Jim's eye. Earlier this week, I thought of Jim's eye when the only cloud in the sky moved behind the water tower, and again when my son's guitar string broke, and then again when my wife waved a yellowjacket away with her hat.

Jim has two eyes: a real eye and a glass eye. He had two real eyes for only six months; an infection in infancy ruined one of them. He has no memory of this ruined eye. The glass eye is realistic. Once he told me how he made his girlfriend vomit by squeezing it out of its socket, then popping it into his mouth. It doesn't move the way the real one does, but it does move a little. It's the little bit of movement that makes it strange.

The remaining real eye: at certain times in my life, I thought about it every day, multiple times a day, even. Even today I worry about it. I worry about Jim losing the real eye—then he would be blind. I don't understand why the thought upsets me so; if Jim had only one kidney, I wouldn't worry about the remaining kidney, even though losing the second kidney would kill him. But I worry about Jim's eye and the possibility that he might go blind.

Something tells me that, even if this did happen, and Jim lost his sight, I would still worry about the eye. Not the actual eye—the *idea* of the eye. And so this is a kind of third eye, an idea-eye that exists independently of both the real one and the glass one. When I think of this eye now, it isn't even part of Jim's face. It's alone, floating in darkness. It doesn't blink, or move in any way, but it still feels alive. It's alive the way my fear is alive.

Jim and I used to be close, but not anymore. He stopped answering my letters ten years ago. I suppose this means that, at this point, we're not even friends. In fact, only since our friendship ended has Jim's eye come to mean so much to me.

Jim, then, was actually an impediment to the relationship: it is the third eye and I who are close now, very close indeed.

Nickname

Her naturally cheerful disposition and unflagging energy, which, in her youth, made her irresistible to family, friends, and even complete strangers, and that began, as she grew into adolescence and then young adulthood, to express itself as a kind of frantic, Pollyannaish desperation, eventually evolved, once she became an adult, into hypomania, obsessive-compulsive behavior, and what her doctor identified as full-blown histrionic personality disorder. Fearful that she was alienating the very people who had once praised her for her winning smile and can-do attitude, she underwent years of intensive therapy, coupled with the ingestion of powerful prescription drugs, rendering herself calm and judicious in all things—only to earn, among her loved ones, a reputation for moroseness, and the nickname "Gloomy Gus."

Lipogram for a Passover Turkey Knife

In days of old, scimitar-swinging warriors struck mighty varmints with skillful swords, slicing in uniform blows until stacks of juicy hunks burnt scrumptiously upon smoky coals. Humans of today lack such manly vigor and cunning know-how. That's why Magna's Compact Victual Cutlass is your handy chum, particularly on holidays and similar important dining occasions, at which unvarying chow width is a must. Call to mind, won't you, Grandma's famous animosity toward nonproportional foodstuffs? A Magna-brand shiv is your crucial tool for maintaining familial harmony on days of holy sup. Buy a Magna now, sit back, and tuck it in without worry. Magna: Sharp Shanks for Choosy Culinarians.

Let Me Think

The father says to the child, Let me think. Because the child is talking—she has been talking all morning—and he just wants to get this one tedious thing finished, and to do so he needs a few minutes of silence. That is all.

The child hesitates, because this is a new command: Let me think. The father is *asking for permission*, a position the child herself is often in. But the child is uncertain how to proceed. This power is new to her. She will have to gather more information. She says, Daddy? What are you doing?

Without turning to look at her, he says, I'm trying to—I'm just— Just, hold on. Just let me think for a minute.

The father is thinking of the ways the child is like her mother: determined—stubborn, even. Selectively, *strategically* oblivious to the obvious, when it suits her needs. He is angry at the child for talking, and he has been angry all morning, though later he will misremember that his outburst, the one he already knows is coming, came *out of nowhere*.

The child would like to let her father think, as he demanded she do; or rather at first she'd wanted to let him think. Now she is wondering if it might be more interesting to withhold the requested permission, to *not* let her father think. How?

She says, Daddy, then considers for a moment what to say next.

Daddy, she says, how are you thinking? Which is not quite the question she meant to ask, and which does not entirely make sense.

Her father says, I'm trying to work!

What he is doing, from the child's perspective, is staring at the screen of a computer. The child understands that this can indeed mean that the father is working, but she knows it can also mean other things. She now doubts the veracity of the father's claim. And while she still doesn't fully understand the mechanism by which control of her father's thoughts rests with her, she does now see that it has something to do with *talking*. What her father wants is for her to *stop talking*. This makes no sense to the child, for talking, to her, is the ultimate form thoughts take, and so is virtually synonymous with thinking. To test this hypothesis, she says, while spinning in place with her arms outstretched, Na na na na na na na na na na—

Shut up! the father screams, wheeling around in his chair, and he reaches for the child, intending to stop her spinning with a firm hand, and compel her to face him squarely. But instead, his hand strikes her face and she falls to the ground. Theatrically! The child theatrically collapses onto the carpet, screeching, after an *obvious* moment of contemplation and calculation!

Later, on the phone with his ex-wife, he will make the mistake of sharing this observation, that their child *pretended* to be hurt, which his ex-wife will recognize as an iteration upon the kind of complaint he often used to levy against her: that she is easily wounded and possessed of an exaggerated sense of injustice—that, indeed, she suffers from a *persecution complex*. She will accuse him, correctly, of applying to his daughter the resentment he still feels toward her, and will threaten to involve their divorce lawyer in the conversation: which is to say, she will implicitly threaten to alter, in the wake of this *borderline abusive act*, their custody agreement. At this point in the conversation, he will take a moment to *let himself think*, and will realize that it is time to *cut his losses* and apologize, which he will do through clenched teeth. After all, he hadn't been working, not really. He had been trying to compose an apologetic email to his lover, the one he left his wife for, and who has proven to be as willful and complicated as both his ex-wife and himself, and who, he now understands, is about to break up with him. (Indeed, even as he forces out his apology to his ex-wife, the breakup email is alighting in his inbox.)

Meanwhile, the child, alone in her room at her house, which is now called *Mommy's house*, will begin to comprehend that it is possible to simultaneously *cultivate a hurt* and *recognize that it is imaginary*, and that these seemingly contradictory states are, in fact, usefully complementary. These will be new thoughts for the child, as will be her resolve, arriving fast in their wake, to *keep them to herself*.

Therapy

You've been in and out of therapy for two years and are not sure if you're supposed to be in therapy. On the one hand, the specific problems you began the therapy to address have been resolved. On the other hand, the process of their resolution has prompted discussion of the forces that caused the problems in the first place, which is ostensibly enlightening and preventative. So maybe you should continue. It is also possible that your doubts about continuing therapy constitute a subject worth examining in therapy. You imagine telling your therapist this, and then you imagine your therapist's expression of mild amusement, which seems to be her reaction to most of what you say. You wonder if, given that you've apparently chosen to remain in therapy, it's a bad idea to invest so much effort in amusing your therapist, or to assume that her look of amusement actually indicates amusement. Don't you already spend enough time trying to amuse people you are not paying for their time? Maybe they're not amused, either. Maybe your need to amuse everyone, including the therapist, is also worth examining in therapy.

Your therapist's office is large, comfortable, and clean. There's a couch, but only in the waiting room, which is much larger than the consulting room, which is where the therapy takes place and which contains only chairs. Your therapist sits in a wheeled office chair, and you sit in an armchair. There's another armchair that remains

empty—presumably it is used for couples therapy. You often imagine that whomever you are talking about in therapy—you're always
talking about somebody or other, and the complexities of their interface with you—is sitting there, nodding as you speak. You imagine
saying things about this person in therapy, then turning to him or
her there in the chair and saying, "Right?" And him or her replying, "Right!" You wonder if your acquaintances would be amused to
know that you have created affirmation-avatar versions of them for
use in the imagined life of your therapy sessions. You think maybe
most of them would. You might be wrong.

You like the therapist's waiting room more than the consulting
room, and sort of wish you could talk in the waiting room instead.
The sofa is comfortable and the building's ventilation system emits a
constant, gently high-pitched tone that randomly fluctuates between
an A-flat and a D. You know this because you once took out your
phone and opened up your electronic synthesizer app to check.
These two notes are a tritone, or augmented fourth, also known as
"the devil's interval." You've never told your therapist this: maybe
you should. It might amuse her. Usually the waiting room is empty
when you arrive and leave, but one day a woman you know, who
works in your building, was sitting on the sofa when you emerged
from the consulting room. You said, "Hi, Susan!" and she smiled
awkwardly. For the next couple of sessions, you found her standing
at the window, her back to the room, as you departed. Presumably
she moved there when she heard you opening the consulting room
door, and returned to the sofa only once you were gone. Not long
after, she changed her appointment time. Now she won't even meet
your gaze at work. Another time, a new client took the slot before
yours; you crossed paths between sessions. She lingered audibly in
the waiting room while you were amusing your therapist in the consulting room, and then she managed to lock herself in the bathroom.
Your therapist had to go help her once the desperate pounding on
the door became too distracting.

Your therapist is a married woman twenty years your senior.
You like her—you share a conversational sensibility and a hobby. You

think she likes you too. In fact you often make the mistake of thinking of her as just some lady you're friends with. You really would
like to be friends with your therapist—it might be preferable to,
and would certainly be cheaper than, your present arrangement, and
would allow you to talk about your common hobby as well—but it's
unlikely that you would have met her outside the present context,
which is to say the paid, as opposed to recreational, sharing of your
innermost thoughts. You have a lot of friends you routinely share
your innermost thoughts with, which, according to your therapist,
is not the norm among her clients. For some reason this flatters you.
A lot of things flatter you. This is either narcissism or evidence of a
healthy interface with the world. The latter possibility, combined
with the freedom you enjoy in sharing your thoughts with friends,
makes you wonder what you need the therapy for. Perhaps this is
another topic worth examining in therapy. You've been in and out
of therapy for two years and are not sure if you're supposed to be in
therapy.

THREE

Winter's Calling

Her phone's ringing. She's awakened by the ringing of her phone. But that can't be right, because she turns her phone off at night. But it's on the bedside table, ringing. She picks it up. The screen's all wrong. It's like a window to someplace where it's winter—a snow scene, a blizzard, really. Winter's calling and she doesn't know how to answer. So she screams, "*Stop*," and that wakes her up and her phone's ringing, not possible because she turns it off at night, but she answers and it's M and he says, "Sarah, are you awake, I have terrible news." She looks out the window by the bed, it's a winter morning, it's snowing, she both knows and doesn't know that Sarah is supposed to be her name, that she's the one the call is for, and she doesn't say, Stop, she says, "I'm up, I'm up, I'm up" and hopes it isn't true.

In Darkness

I went to the woodshed without a flashlight and stood there quietly, in the slight depression the hens had made as they bathed in dust and sun, waiting for my eyes to adjust and for the woodpile to come into view.

Instead, the darkness deepened. No cars passed on the nearby road. Features of the scene before me that I knew to be real—the chaotically tidy face of the wood I had stacked months before, and the oblique slant of the rafters above it—swam in and out of view, but when I closed my eyes, they continued to pitch and swoon, and I knew I was imagining them.

My senses were dulled by flu. When I coughed, the sound seemed to come not from my own body, but from something nearby and underwater.

Do you remember, in childhood, being gripped and shaken by the sea? Lifted from your feet, twisted, driven into the sand . . . Yes, you remember the fear, but do you remember the relief? Everything has been taken away, and you are entirely at the mercy of something. Anything could happen now. Maybe, soon, your body will be returned to you; maybe it will be the same as before. Maybe not. There's nothing you can do. The ocean and the ocean's floor will decide.

Eventually, bored of myself, I gathered the firewood in darkness.

The Cottage on the Hill (II)

The next time Richard returned to the cottage was eight years later, when his daughter, Lila, was a teenager, and his son, Greg, an adolescent. He and Evelyn had been divorced for some years, their parting acrimonious and irreconcilable. The two hadn't spoken since they separated, and even took care, whenever they exchanged the children, not to enter into the other's line of sight. Evelyn would put the children on a bus to Richard's apartment, and after a few days Richard dropped them off a block from Evelyn's house, making sure each time that her front door opened to admit them before he drove away.

He didn't get along with the children. Evelyn, he believed, had poisoned their minds against him. As far as he knew, he might have done the same to her; it was difficult to conceal from his children his distaste for their mother, even in the best of circumstances. In any event, he was inclined to blame himself as much as he blamed her for his problems with Lila and Greg.

It was his guilt that led him to investigate the possibility of spending a few days with the children at the cottage. Perhaps they would remember the fun they had had there; perhaps their relationship with their father could, to some extent, be repaired. It took an hour of riffling through old papers to discover the phone number of the substation, and it was with a sense of real triumph and optimism that he called. But instead of the crisp gas company salutation, all he heard on the end of the line was a glum, slurred hello.

"I'm sorry, is this the gas company substation?"

"Nope."

"Pardon me. Is this 535-9912?"

"Yeah. It used to be the gas company, now it ain't."

It was the voice of a woman, tired and perhaps drunk. Richard apologized for bothering her. "Do you happen to know the gas company's new number?"

After a pause, the voice said, "They're long gone. It's us here now. The place was converted."

For a moment, Richard was uncertain what she meant. Then, "You mean the substation?" he said.

"Yeah."

"So you're . . ." He struggled to understand. "It's the same place as before, then. At the bottom of the hill. And you live there now?"

"Yep."

Richard cleared his throat. "I was actually calling . . . Well, I must ask you, is the cottage still there? On the hill?"

There was another pause, longer this time, as though the woman were reaching far back into her memory. "Oh, sure. Sure, that's still there." Suddenly her voice took on some enthusiasm. "You want to rent it, is that it?"

"Well . . . that's what I'd hoped. But if it's out of repair . . ."

"Oh, no, you can have it, it's just fine. I can send Ted up there to get it ready. No, it's fine, available for rent and everything." The woman was quite excited now, talking more quickly, seeming to be thinking out loud. "Oh, I can wash those curtains . . . and maybe give it a quick coat of paint. And firewood, we'll have to haul some firewood up there . . ."

"Really," Richard said, "I don't want to be a bother. If the place isn't habitable anymore, I really . . ."

"Oh, it's habitable. Oh, it's habitable."

"Well, that's very good news. Ah . . . but . . . I was thinking of coming up in just a few days. Sunday, to be precise."

"Sunday!" A bit of doubt seemed to enter the woman's voice, but it was quickly dispelled. "Oh, that's no trouble at all, sir, no trouble! I'll just send Ted up there right away! And we'll get you some clean sheets and fill up the fridge with good things to eat."

"That's not necessary . . ."

"Maybe some fresh bread and lunch meat and what have you," the woman said, "and a nice bowl of fruit. Nothing makes a place seem homey like a bowl of fruit, wouldn't you say?" There was no arguing with her—in the end Richard was forced to go ahead and book the cottage for three days.

When he told the children where they would be spending the weekend together, Greg shrugged—he had no recollection of the cottage and didn't seem to care what they did. Lila crossed her arms and scowled. "Fine," she said, as if the trip were some kind of punishment.

On the way to the cottage, Greg fell asleep in the back seat while Lila sat, arms still crossed, on the passenger side, occasionally glaring at Richard with disarming steadiness and anger. "What is it?" he asked her, several times, and it was only on the third try that she replied, "You know."

"I don't."

"I wish you'd just come out with it," she said. "*Dad.*" This term of endearment was uttered with such venom that for a moment Richard had to stifle a deep sigh. What had he done wrong?

Richard drove past the former substation twice before he recognized it: everything had changed. The chain-link fence was gone, and, despite what the woman had said, the cinder block building had been replaced by a trailer, the sort that usually serves as a temporary office on a construction site. The only evidence that this had ever been a gas company facility was a cluster of disused, rusted iron pipes sticking out of the ground at the edge of the lot. The lot itself was overgrown with weeds, and an old pickup truck was parked in a pair of tire ruts.

It was with some trepidation that Richard knocked on the trailer door. The woman who answered was not as he'd expected—she was younger, for one thing, close to his own age. And she was quite attractive—glamorous, even. She wore a gingham dress and a bobbed hairdo, like a woman of the distant past. "Well, I sure hope you all have a wonderful time," she said. "Ted's up there now, just finishing."

"I appreciate that," Richard said. "We're hoping to go for a row on the lake."

Her face darkened. "Not sure what you'll find down there. Something, anyway."

"Of course."

Now the woman seemed evasive, and sounded more the way she had when she answered the phone, tired and old. She withdrew a few inches into the trailer. "I guess you'll be wanting to get up there, then . . . ," she said.

"But where's the road?" Richard asked. Because the dirt track that had once led to the cottage seemed no longer to be there.

"Road? You can't drive up there. Is that what you mean?"

It was true, the hillside did appear steeper than before, and was strewn with rocks and wild shrubs. Perhaps he'd misremembered the drive up the hill, years before. He turned back to the woman to tell her this, but she had disappeared, and the door had closed. A small, faded sign on it read ONTEO ENERGY.

Richard and the children gathered their suitcases and sack of food and began the long trudge up the muddy hillside. Several times each of them slipped and dropped their possessions. Greg banged his knee against a rock, and Lila seemed to be muttering something under her breath.

When at last they reached the top, it was nearly dark. The cottage was not as he recalled. The tree was still there, but the structure itself was lower, broader. The clapboards were wider, and painted a peeling white, and the second floor seemed to be missing entirely. Furthermore, the view on the far side was drastically different. The lake he remembered was gone—only a weedy marsh seemed to lie in the valley below, and the hills did not appear as tall as they once had. Indeed, if they were there at all, they were obscured by fog. He began to feel a terrible sense of dread.

His thoughts were interrupted by a hearty hello from a middle-aged man with a pronounced limp, who emerged from beneath the eaves of the cottage. He wore bib overalls and a bushy gray beard. It was hard to imagine him as the woman's husband—perhaps they were related some other way.

"Got it all ready for you, sir," he said, frowning.

"It looks quite different," Richard told him. "I thought I remembered a second floor."

The man shook his head. "Wasn't one when we bought it."

"It looks like an entirely different cottage, actually."

But the man didn't seem to want to talk; indeed, he appeared thoroughly disgusted with Richard, the cottage, and the entire situation. Then he looked over Richard's shoulder and seemed to catch sight of something. Richard turned. Only the children stood there, staring at the ground.

"Those your kids?"

"Yes, they are."

"Well, we don't allow no kids here."

"Your wife told me nothing of the sort. I wouldn't have made the reservation if she had."

"We don't like the noise," the man went on.

"But there's nothing for miles around!"

"Sound travels." He stared at the ground, exhaled through his nose like a bull. "Goddammit. We'll make an exception this time. Just tell 'em to keep the noise down. Evelyn has a condition." And he turned and disappeared below the curve of the hill.

As it happened, the inside of the cottage was familiar, after all. The kitchen cabinets were the same, and the paneling, and the old photos of the expressionless people. The bedrooms were the same too—although they were even smaller than Richard remembered, the walls nearly touching the beds on all sides, and had somehow been moved to the lower floor. Luckily, there was a television, and Lila and Greg were able to watch movies all evening as Richard tried to read a book. At one point a phone rang, and there was a comical search for it; they finally found it improbably hung inside a cabinet. It was Ted, asking them to turn the TV down. But by this time, the

children were tired, and decided to simply switch the set off and go
to sleep.

Richard woke during the night to the sound of whispering, coming through the wall behind his head. *What if he comes in?* said one
voice—Lila's, he thought.

I won't let him.

He's bigger than you.

I could kill him if I had to.

In the morning, he wasn't certain he had heard the conversation
at all.

By the middle of the following afternoon, it was clear that the trip
had been a mistake. The children wouldn't talk to him, except to ask
him repeatedly if they could go home. He convinced them to take a
walk down to the marsh, in the hope that they might find a hiking
path or creek, but there were only stinging insects and a foul odor,
and they were forced to climb back up the hill, becoming dirty and
sweaty as they did so. The last straw came while Richard was standing alone, looking out over the depressing landscape, and heard a
shuffling behind him. It was Lila.

"Hi, sweetie," he said.

"Why don't you just do it and get it over with," she said. Her
voice trembled and there were tears in her eyes.

"Do what? I don't understand."

"I hate you!" she shouted, and stormed off down the hill toward
the road.

In the end, he decided that there was no point in staying. He and
Greg gathered their things, closed up the cottage, and set off down
the hill. They found Lila already sitting in the car, fast asleep. Richard
knocked on the door to tell the strange couple they were leaving, but
they weren't home. Indeed, the place looked abandoned—through
the window, nothing could be seen but a desk, a filing cabinet, some
forgotten office supplies.

He drove back to town and dropped off the children one block
from their mother's house.

Unnamed

You are in a truck moving downhill past a red-and-white sign on a metal pole that shows a truck moving downhill through a feature-less white landscape. You pass a woman walking your way, bent back slightly to compensate for the hill; you think you should offer her a ride. In the side-view mirror her blurred face is raised, and your own blurred face looks back at you alongside her, and you think you'll come back and find her after you've reached your destination, what-ever it is, and are returning to where you came from, wherever it is.

But you don't know where you are, or where you are going, and nothing you have seen has appeared ever again, except for the sign depicting a truck, your truck, moving downhill into the blurred brown and blue, which has repeated itself every few miles, as though to remind you, to *warn* you, that you're in a truck moving down-hill, again, still.

The woman is gone now, lost in dust. Ahead is the fog that is the future, and there is only straight and down. There is another sign, and then another.

The road has no name. This is the commonest name in the world for a road.

Monsters

The blind man, who everyone agreed was exceedingly handsome and who had married a woman widely regarded, among their acquaintances, as extraordinarily beautiful, was chosen to participate in the trial of a new medical procedure that doctors believed might fully restore sight to certain patients. The surgery was a complete success, but when the handsome man saw, for the first time, his own face and the face of his wife, he was horrified, and could not be dissuaded of the notion that they, and everyone around them, were hideous monsters; and when, six months later, the procedure's efficacy unexpectedly faded, and the handsome man was plunged again into darkness, he said that he was not, as his friends might have predicted, relieved, but rather more horrified still, because now, and forevermore, he could not know with any certainty where the monsters were.

The Unsupported Circle

An overhead shot, evidently from a camera drone, of a large number of men and women standing in the sun. Their business-casual
attire, and position upon a neatly mowed patch of grass surrounded
by parking lots, suggest that they are the employees of a small company. They are arranged, front to back, in a tight queue that curves
around to meet itself.

A disembodied male voice, amplified as though through a mega-
phone, counts down from three. On two, the employees square their
shoulders. On one, they raise their hands into the air. And when
the voice says, "Now!" they all bend their knees and fall back, each
settling onto the newly created lap of the employee behind them.

The circle wobbles but holds. Every person is seated. A wild cheer
goes up.

○

A teenage boy wearing a backwards baseball cap and a heavily laden
backpack is freestyling to an improvised beatboxing rhythm, presumably provided by the person filming. The boy is walking as he
raps, swinging his arms in generous arcs and waving finger-guns at
the cameraman. His rap is about his superiority to other rappers. It's
a sunny day, and in the background, across the street, a woman is
pushing a baby in a stroller. Just after the four-second mark, a shape

appears on the leading edge of the screen. It's a street sign. The teenage boy walks into it, and its thin aluminum corner gouges his forehead. Just before his hands reach his face, blood can be seen pouring out of the wound. The boy screams as the cameraman's beatboxing trails off into hoarse, uncontrolled laughter. In the background, the woman stops walking, in apparent shock. The stroller continues rolling down the sidewalk ahead of her.

The scene changes to a hospital room, where the rapper lies in bed, wincing as a nurse cleans his wound with a small square of gauze. "Bro, don't film this," he says, raising his open palm to the camera. "Bro, don't. Bro."

○

Night. An industrial area: distant, cold streetlight behind a chain-link fence; weedy, flat, graveled ground; a cinder block wall illuminated by flashlights. One flashlight belongs to a young woman in a hoodie, whom we see from behind, illuminated by a second flashlight. The young woman is creeping forward, toward the wall and the darkness beyond it. Crickets can be heard, the crunch of footsteps, the hiss of a distant highway. The young woman scans the darkness, her blond ponytail twitching.

The young woman reaches the wall. The darkness opens before her. She stands straight; her flashlight beam sweeps the broken ground.

A second figure appears, screaming, from behind the wall: a person wearing a mask. The mask is the face of a witch or old hag: sharp chin, long nose, sinister grin. The mask-wearer seems to be a young man, dressed in jeans and a flannel shirt; he has his own flashlight, which he's using to illuminate the mask.

The young woman does not react. Instead, after a beat, she and the witch both turn their heads in response to a noise from the gloom to the left. An instant later, a third person leaps out of the dark, with their own flashlight and mask, this one a caricature, vaguely racist, of then president Barack Obama. It's another young man, also in jeans and flannel.

Again, the young woman does not react. Instead, the witch-boy screams in fear, then punches the Obama-boy in the face. The two begin to grapple, and soon tumble into the blackness, pummeling each other with their fists.

The young woman turns to face the camera. Her face is pale, moonlike. She stares, expressionless, into the light.

o

An elderly woman is sitting in an armchair, reading the newspaper. A child's voice says, "Grandma, do it!"

"No, child, leave me alone," the woman says.

"Do it!" a second child cries.

"C'mon, Grandma, do it! Do it!"

"Go away," the woman says.

"Grandmaaaaaa!"

"Grandma, please? Please do it, Grandma."

"I will not."

"Please?"

"Please, Grandma."

The elderly woman lays down the newspaper in her lap. A single headline is visible, on a turned-down corner: ZONING DISPUTE LEADS TO STABBING. She tilts her head back slightly and opens her mouth wide: so preternaturally wide that it appears, for a moment, as though something—some small, oily monster or wispy spirit-thing—might suddenly emerge. Instead, with a jerking, heaving motion, she emits a series of caws, shockingly loud and uncannily authentic. For these seconds, she has been possessed by, has actually become, a crow.

The unseen children howl in terror as the elderly woman's face returns to normal. She takes up her newspaper while the children continue to scream. Behind her, framed by the window, a mail truck passes through the bright day.

o

A shaky, zoomed-in shot of a tightly packed group of people on a suburban porch, holding drinks, laughing, and talking. It's a party:

they're noisy, but far enough away that the sound is muddled and vague, like a rainstorm.

Instead, the audio is dominated by the person behind the camera, who is muttering, "How dare they. How *dare* they. *How dare they.*"

○

A child dressed in colonial-style frock coat, vest, and tricorn hat is standing in front of a farm field, reciting a portion of Patrick Henry's "Give me liberty, or give me death!" speech. The child—long-faced and mournful, not unlike popular depictions of the real Patrick Henry—is struggling with the speech, and is repeatedly prompted by the adult behind the camera.

"Why stand we here . . . evil?"

"Idle."

"Why stand here we . . . why we stand here idle? What is it that gentlemen wish? Is life so . . . so . . ."

"Is life so dear."

"Is life so dear, or sweet so . . . or sweet . . ."

"Or peace so sweet . . ."

". . . as to be purchased by the chains of . . . the price of . . ."

The child is interrupted by a noise, and turns to his left. In response to something he sees off-screen, he shouts, "Billy, no!" The camera follows his eyes, revealing, in the grass several feet away, a colorful rooster in the act of copulating with a hen. The hen wears an expression of patient endurance and has, clutched in her beak, a single large pancake.

○

I remember watching this one with you. A weathered wooden door, interrupting a shingled wall and bisected diagonally into light and shade, creaks open, and a hand appears in the gap a few inches from the top of the jamb. There is something wrong with the hand, though it's hard at first to apprehend what. The hand grips the door and pushes it open farther; we expect a person to emerge, headfirst.

And a head does poke out through the opening, and it's wrong, too: it's upside down. It belongs to a middle-aged, bearded man, who is dangling from some unseen platform or handhold inside the house, in an attempt to startle the cameraman with his unorthodox orientation.

The trick works. The cameraman gasps, and the scene wobbles as the man drops down into the gloom with a grin. You gasped, too, every time—even though we sat and watched it together again and again.

o

Several dozen yards beyond a heavy black wrought iron fence, a man in a suit is emerging from a Greek Revival building—some courthouse or seat of government—pursued by a cluster of reporters and photographers. From the vicinity of the camera, another man's voice shouts, "Senator! Senator!"

The senator continues to descend the steps, but looks up at the camera.

"Fuck you, Senator! Murderer! You killed my wife! Fuck you, you monster!"

The senator raises a hand in evident acknowledgment of the comments. Heavy footsteps can be heard, distantly at first, then near. The scene flashes, wheels, turns into blur. For a fraction of a second, the tumbling camera shows a man, in perhaps early middle age, wearing a windbreaker and black slacks, being tackled by two police officers, a man and a woman.

With a rumble and a scrape, the scene stabilizes. The camera now faces blue sky, across which a bough of azalea, brightly in bloom, extends. A bee alights upon a blossom.

o

A small bird stomps majestically across a linoleum floor.

o

An unrenovated basement room. The concrete foundation, painted white, bears the marks of the plywood forms that gave it its shape. A single small window at the upper right shows a neighboring roofline, a strip of blue sky through which gray clouds move. In the half-cylinder window well, formed from black corrugated plastic, a cat is curled in sleep.

In front of the white concrete wall stands a boy about ten years old, wearing a top hat and cape and holding a white-tipped black magic wand. In front of the boy stands a small table covered with props; children and adults are seated on folding chairs facing it.

The video has been transferred from an obsolete magnetic-tape format, perhaps MiniDV, and edited into its current form. Long rectangles of solid digital color flicker periodically near the edges of the screen, and a gray line appears and vanishes at the bottom. The stability of the image suggests that the camera is affixed to a tripod, but the edits are obvious by the sudden changes in the posture of the subjects. Each scene depicts an attempt at a magic trick:

1. The magician shakes the wand, pauses, shakes it again. Its tip pops off and a single silk rose, partly deformed by its residence in the black plastic tube, slides out and falls to the ground.

2. The arm of a smaller boy, perhaps the magician's brother, has been inserted into a miniature guillotine, which the magician now snaps shut. The smaller boy, obviously unharmed, nevertheless tumbles to the floor and begins to roll around screaming, smashing the toy guillotine against the concrete. "Stop!" the magician implores him, to the laughter of the crowd.

3. The magician tries, and fails, to pronounce the word "abracadabra."

4. The magician removes his hat, attempting to prevent the plush bird underneath it from slipping out, but it slips out.

Finally, the magician announces that he will disappear. He sweeps his cape up over his face. The scene abruptly changes once more, this

time to the basement room empty of people, the magic props un-
disturbed on the table. Even the cat in the window well is gone.

○

The highway outside a moving car is eerily illuminated by an other-
worldly glow of uncertain origin. We are looking through the windshield; the subtle canting of the image, to the left and right, suggests
that the driver is using the steering wheel to stabilize their phone,
and making slight adjustments to keep the car in its lane. A song by
Taylor Swift is playing on the radio, and the dashboard is cluttered
with objects: an empty or nearly empty cigarette packet; a plastic
water bottle, lying on its side; a pair of sunglasses; a half-eaten roll
of Life Savers candy.

The right edge of the screen brightens until the entire sky is obscured by clipped highlights. Then the camera adjusts, darkening the
scene and revealing an enormous fast-moving object—a meteorite,
no doubt—streaking at an oblique angle, right to left, across our field
of vision. It is a yellowish ball of light trailed by a long tail of glowing
smoke and debris. On the highway in the distance, brake lights flash.

Then the object passes off the screen at lower left, and the scene
abruptly darkens, revealing that it is nighttime. Stars emerge in the
purple sky. Someone, the driver, draws breath and begins to let out
what might be a sob—but the video cuts out before the sound can
resolve.

○

Loud hip-hop music plays at a crowded poolside party attended by
muscled young white men in knee-length swimming trunks and
tanned, bikini-clad young white women. The pool is large and
placid and illuminated from underneath; people stand in it, cock-
tails and beers in hand, and one person floats on an inflatable raft,
gazing at the glow from her phone. A cluster of revelers stands near
a drinks cart decorated in tiki style, among them a slim girl with
golden hair as straight and even as the harp of a piano, and with the
erect and formal posture of a palace guard.

Only on repeated viewings is one likely to notice the crew-cutted boy creeping up behind her, clutching a dark object. He pauses, concealed partly by the bodies of partygoers and partly by a flowering shrub, then lurches forward, encircling the girl's waist with his tattooed arms, folding her up like a letter, and pulling her down with him into the pool.

The easygoing drinkers react with screams. The raft passenger startles so violently that she capsizes, thrusting her phone into the air quickly enough to protect it from the water. The tackler and tackled resurface together, and before the girl can push her sopping hair back from her face, the boy shoves a small black box in front of her eyes and opens it. A small white dot, barely more than a pixel, can be discerned inside. *"Chloe will you marry me!"* the boy bellows.

She rears back to reflexive oohs from the crowd. The crack of her palm as it strikes his cheek is audible even through the pumping bass.

○

Some cows are standing in a field, intermingled with some sheep. At the same time that a goat enters from the right, pulling grass from the ground with its teeth, a golden retriever lopes into the scene from the bottom of the frame. Then a cat trots in impassively from the left, followed, startlingly, by a male peacock, its tail fanned in apparent appeal to an off-screen hen.

There is a pause, during which it seems as though the gathering of animals has ended. Then a V of geese appears in the sky, emitting a chorus of honks.

The goat looks up—not at the geese, but rather as though its phone were buzzing in its pocket.

○

A woman is balancing two teetering stacks of teacups and saucers, five cups and five saucers in each outstretched hand. The cups, decorated in a grandmotherly pattern of flowering vines, appear to be filled to the brim with milky tea; it splashes over the rims of the two top cups. The woman is in some kind of windowless community space, a church basement or village hall, surrounded by enthusiastic onlookers. Empty folding chairs stand at haphazard angles to round wood-veneer tables, as though the onlookers have suddenly taken to their feet in excitement. Upon the concrete floor, a perfect circle, about five feet in diameter, has been described in masking tape; the teacup-bearer traces the tape circle in short, precise steps, like a windup toy. Her gaze flicks from her feet to the left stack to the right stack. Her mouth is curled into a small, determined smile.

The woman's progress is accompanied by a rising chorus of ahhs from the onlookers. A few people raise their hands to their faces in apprehension; one man, at the far right edge of the screen, can be seen to have inserted almost his entire fist into his mouth. When the cup-bearer has completed the full circle, the video ends and then restarts, in a nearly seamless loop. The angle of the woman's face, the position of her hands and feet: it's all perfect. The illusion of infinity is complete.

I wanted to google—*woman teacups circle*—for the inevitable uncut video, where the woman drops the teacups and they splash and shatter on the floor, but you wouldn't let me. Why ruin it? you said.

Much later, when we were no longer together, I did it. I googled the video. You were right: I ruined it.

Marriage (Coffee)

She says, We're out of coffee. I'm going out.

We're not out of coffee, he says. I just bought coffee.

That stuff you bought, she says, isn't coffee.

Respectfully, he says, yes, it is. It's the exact coffee we've been drinking for the past five years. You drink this coffee literally every day.

I haven't drunk it in ages.

Every morning, he says, I brew a pot of this very coffee and pour some into a mug and bring it to you in bed. And you lie in bed and read and you drink this exact coffee.

Well, she says, I appreciate the gesture, I really do. But the fact is, I don't drink it.

Just yesterday I watched you drink it. You raised the mug to your lips and gave me a little wave.

Yes. I raised it to my lips; then, when you left the room, I got out of bed, went to the bathroom sink, and poured it down the drain.

I don't get it, he says. You love coffee.

Not this coffee, she says. I go to the coffee shop on Seventh. They source their beans from small farms in Latin America, Africa, and Southeast Asia. Then they roast them on the premises. The roaster is from Milan. He earns seventy-five thousand a year. They grind the coffee in precision burr grinders and pour pure, hot water over the grounds by hand. That's the only coffee I've drunk since 2011.

Why didn't you tell me? he says.

I didn't want to make you feel bad.

But now I feel even worse. I feel like a fool.

He goes on: The roaster, he says. From Milan.

Yes?

Is he good-looking?

Very, she says.

Better-looking than me?

Of course.

After a moment, he asks, Are you sleeping with him?

Only once, she says. He has a lot of sex. I'm actually surprised he agreed to it.

It was your idea?

She nods.

How did that work, exactly? You accepted the coffee from him and said, Would you like to have sex with me?

The roaster doesn't do the pour-over. That's the barista. Don't you know anything? Anyway, I didn't proposition him at his workplace. That would be harassment. I did it in a bar.

He says, Was it one of those nights you said you were going out with Lisa?

There is no Lisa, she says.

I see. So, I should stop buying this coffee, then.

No, keep buying it! You like it.

Actually, he says, I don't. I bought it because I thought you liked it. I've been sitting in the kitchen every morning drinking this coffee because I imagined that you were lying in bed drinking it too. I figured, even though we don't like to be together in the morning, we could at least drink the same drink. Actually, he says, I prefer tea. Or juice, even. I'm more of a tea and juice man.

That's so sweet, she says.

Yeah.

Do you want to come with me now? she says. You could meet Federico.

I don't know, he says.

You'd like him. He's kind of an asshole.

Yeah?

Yeah.

This time, they go to the coffee shop together.

Marriage (Dogs)

Years ago, he said, I want a dog, and she said, No, no dogs, you can have a dog with your second wife. At a different time, also years ago, she said, Maybe we should have a dog, and he said, Well, I am not going to live with a dog, so you'll have to choose between a dog and me.

Each recalls his or her own dog request as predating the other's. Each recalls his or her own dog objection as having been gentle and perfunctory. And so one day, when she impulsively adopts a dog from the shelter, he responds by going out and adopting a dog from the shelter.

Each dislikes the other's dog. The dogs dislike each other. She even secretly dislikes her own dog, who smells terrible, even after a bath, and he secretly dislikes his own dog, who has a habit of eating things that are not food. But each feigns adoration of his or her own dog.

Neither is willing to so much as speak the name of the other's dog. They say things like:

Get your fucking dog off of the bed.

Your fucking dog is in my closet. Get the dog out of the fucking closet.

This fucking dog smells like a pile of shit.

This dog needs a walk. Walk this fucking dog.

Because neither will help fulfill the other's dog's needs, many redundant chores are undertaken, like walks, trips to the vet and to the supermarket for dog food, and the cleaning up of messes. Some messes are of unknown origin, as they are created while both humans are out of the house, and so each blames the other's dog and refuses to clean the messes up. She and he rarely see each other, and when they do it is in the context of coincidental dog-related effort.

The dogs bark all night, at each other and at passing dogs outside. Eventually a neighbor complains: Your dogs are waking up my dogs. You have to quiet your dogs.

Mind your own fucking business, she tells the neighbor.

Her husband agrees. We're not responsible, he says, for what your goddamn dogs do.

Our dogs are the best, she goes on.

Try training your own goddamn dogs, he adds.

That night, they have sex for the first time in three months, while their dogs whine, bark, and growl at this unfamiliar and inexplicable act.

The following day they return the dogs to the shelter. They say:

These dogs you gave us are out of control.

They're dangerous dogs.

Whoever had these dogs before us were psychopaths.

Those people have damaged these dogs irreparably.

As if to illustrate these points, the two dogs bark and snarl in rage and confusion.

No further pets are brought into the marriage, though months pass before the dog food, dog bowls, and dog toys are thrown away. In a few years, the entire episode is forgotten by everyone but the neighbor.

Marriage (Whiskey)

When he gets home, she is sitting on the sofa, holding a bottle of whiskey.

I've decided to try drinking, she says.

Drinking? he asks her. Why?

We're complacent. Blandly happy. It's time for a change.

We're not happy at all, he says.

I'm sick of everything being comfortable and easy, she says, taking a deep swig from the bottle. I'm shaking things up.

Things are very hard, he says. We live in an environment of complete emotional chaos.

Don't you want a little risk in your life? she says. A little drama? There's no drama around here, she says, drinking.

No, I don't. I don't want any drama.

Have some, she says, offering him the bottle.

No, he says. He's still standing by the door, in his running sneakers, holding a briefcase.

It's vile. Seriously. It cost eight dollars.

Are you drunk yet? he asks.

Yes.

Do you like it?

That's not the point, she says. The point is that alcohol ruins lives.

I'm trying to bring ruin down upon us. Eight dollars is a small price to pay for that.

We've been ruined for some time, he observes.

He goes to the bedroom, takes off his shoes, and lies down. He reads some things on the internet about coping with an alcoholic spouse. Then he watches some videos about ghosts, and some videos of people falling down and getting hit by things. He looks at some pictures of girls' breasts. He hears her climbing the stairs and entering the bathroom, and then he hears the sound of vomiting.

He gets up off the bed, goes into the bathroom, and sits on the floor beside her. The room reeks of cheap booze. It's the smell of ruined lives. He pats her on the back as she throws up.

Stop that, she says. It's annoying.

I love you very much, he says.

It's not me you love, she says, wiping snot and saliva from her face, and gazing blearily into his eyes. It's my sickness.

The Regulations

Our job was to drive to airports, high schools, bus garages, and other municipal facilities, to find the closet or cabinet where the cans and bottles of chemicals were kept, and to read the contents of those cans and bottles aloud into miniature tape recorders. Within a few weeks, a pool of secretaries would transcribe the tapes onto adhesive labels, with which we would return to the facility in question, where we would locate the cans and bottles whose contents we had recorded. We would remove the adhesive labels from their paper backings and carefully stick them on top of the lists of contents we had used to generate the tapes.

When we pointed out to our supervisor that, far be it from us to question the usefulness of our work, but didn't the entire process seem to him wasteful and unnecessary, he shook his head and responded, "It's regulations." Our supervisor was a bearish man with a long black-and-gray beard and a great belly that advanced before him like a keg of beer he was carrying through a crowd at a party. People stepped aside for him, in spite of themselves. He was aggressive, officious, and dismissive, yet he was also charming. With the exception of his son, who worked alongside us during our labeling expeditions, we all tried unsuccessfully to curry favor with him in the mornings, when we received our assignments, and this left us all feeling ashamed and subdued on the long drive to our destination.

In any event, the regulations our supervisor referred to really did prescribe this obscure process. These regulations had been generated by our supervisor's father, when he'd worked for a state government agency that oversaw workplace safety. When our supervisor's father retired, he founded our company, which was dedicated to upholding the regulations he had created as a younger man; and now his son had shouldered the yoke of the regulations that were, apparently, his birthright.

Further complicating this arrangement was the fact that our supervisor's son had no interest in, or respect for, regulations at all, the ones his grandfather had created or any others, as far as we could tell. He showed up late to work, smoked and drank on the job, treated our clients rudely, and generally made everyone's lives more difficult. He was fond of calling all site custodians "Vic" regardless of their real names, and liked to perform what all of us had to admit, with deep misgivings, was a masterful impersonation of his father: head and shoulders thrown back, he would waddle up to building officials like a man twice his age and weight, and start barking orders about the regulations, how the regulations needed to be followed, and so please lead us to the closets and cabinets that contained the chemicals, so that we could regulate them with our regulations immediately, am I making myself clear, Vic? You could practically see the belly and beard, so strongly was their presence implied. The custodians tended to be a dispassionate bunch, and generally ignored our supervisor's son's antics, and before long we would find ourselves back before the rows of cans and bottles, either dictating their contents into our recorders or obscuring the list of contents with labels bearing lists of the contents.

That was in 1989. I was recently back in my home town, attending the funeral of a friend, and found myself driving past the strip mall where the workplace safety company's headquarters had been housed. I was surprised to find the blandly familiar sign still in the window, and I stopped in to say hello to our supervisor, who I assumed must still be working there, if the company was still in business.

And indeed he was, beard and belly intact, as officious as ever, and strangely well preserved given his obvious poor health. I spoke familiarly with him for a few minutes before he mentioned that his father had died.

I was startled by this revelation, because I thought that the old man had been dead for years—since before I worked for the company, in fact. It was then that I realized I was speaking not to my supervisor, but to his once-wayward son, who resembled perfectly the 1989 iteration of the father, now deceased. It was, in fact, as though the son's impersonation had extended into the realm of body morphology; the virtual belly and beard had become real, and the waddling, pushy walk had lost its comic exaggeration. It was just the way he walked now. I baited the son about changes to the laws regulating chemical use in municipal structures, hoping he would launch into his jokey routine about "the regulations," but instead he responded in earnest, having apparently accepted the ancestral legislation without irony, and explained that the regulations still necessitated the application of labels. He gestured behind him, toward the pool of now greatly aged secretaries, with their headphones and outdated computers; a bank of laser printers spat out sheets of labels. I could see, even from across the room, that they still bore the familiar ingredients: the petroleum distillates, the hydrocarbons, the perchloroethylene and glycol ethers. Doubtless, a team of college students would soon be dispatched to affix them to bottles and cans—perhaps the new supervisor's own disrespectful son or daughter among them.

I didn't wait to find out. I was in town for a funeral, after all, and used it now as an excuse to withdraw from the workplace safety compliance office with an insincere promise to stop by again someday when I had more time. A few hours later, after the burial, I found myself in my friend's home, surrounded by flowers and casseroles, gently embracing the widow, whom I had dated for some months before my friend met her, and whose comely daughter had just entered the room via the stairs, looking, in her sadness, much as my friend's wife had when she dumped me for my friend in 1987;

and in the mirror behind her as she hesitantly approached, I saw my own face, a stranger's, beholding itself and the daughter with trepidation and confusion.

My life, the one I'd left this town to make for myself, felt far away, little more than a dim, doorless room across which the past and future faced each other, infinitely repeating. So I kissed my friend's widow, waved gamely to her daughter, and headed for the door. But the crowd pressed closer, and pushed me back, and I was drawn deeper and deeper into the wake.

#facultyretreat

The morning of the faculty retreat. The location has just been revealed to us, via courier. We arrive sweating, aroused.

Professor Smenkins proposes mandatory sunlight-sensitivity training. The grumbling is causing the croissant tray to vibrate.

Professor Chen-Velasquez appears to be levitating the conference table with her mind.

Are Professors Nelson and Underbridge playing footsie? They are sitting fourteen feet apart. And yet it seems to be so.

Professor Gutierrez is delivering his remarks in French and everyone is pretending to understand.

Professor Van der Hoet keeps flickering in and out of view, like a distant rare deer seen through trees.

Games of trust: Completing one another's grant applications. Blindfolded peer review. Intercommittee hand-holding. Musical chairs.

Professors on sabbatical are represented at the table by service animals. Professor Abata is purring. Professor Kimmel needs to go walkies.

Professor Umber, impassioned, fist pounding the table: "We must give the dean a hotfoot! The dean must receive a hotfoot!!"

We file out into the side garden for a participatory presentation called "Angercise It!"

The Subcategories Committee is bifurcating. More committees, within committees, some staffed by fractions of professors.

Professors Nelson and Underbridge have not moved from their seats but have somehow progressed to kissing. Their mouths move, fish-like, in sync.

Heavy use of "collapse" as a transitive verb. Sporadic nodding/clapping. Conjuring the spirits of dead lecturers. Hiccuping.

A fight has broken out over the department softball team uniforms. Every color combination evokes a different genocide.

Professor Hsu has escaped! We arm the adjuncts with poison darts. "Bring us her head and your contracts will be renewed."

Our problem is brand recognition. We'll hire a publicist. Our logo will feature corduroy, mirrors, antidepressants, the email REPLY-ALL button.

An incursion into the chemistry retreat has rewarded us with a terrified associate. We theorize him, hungrily, breathlessly.

We supplement the cross-listing of courses with bi-listing, inter-listing, de-listing, meta-listing, ur-listing, non-listing.

Lunch break. Twin vats of gray-green slurry, one marked NUTRITIVE, the other, NON-NUTRITIVE. Tuxedoed attendants wink.

Professor Vliet adheres to the ceiling. He hisses. Bits of his exoskeleton flake off, rain down upon the buffet cart.

After lunch, someone mentions the students. A horrified silence descends, then is broken by Professor Li's mad cackle.

"Troubling," Professor Evans mutters from behind his mask, dice rattling in his bony hand. "I am troubled. Troubled."

Professor Baggs proposes burrowing beneath the building to create new office space. The canvas sack of trowels clatters open.

We pause in our discussion of criteria for the major to allow Professors Nelson and Underbridge to climax. Mild applause.

"Onus," Professor Samson says oilily. "Say it with me. Onus." We utter the word, an incantation. We are a hive, a swarm.

The faculty retreat is winding down. Professor Os has donned her cowl. Professor Burden's keys jingle. The room fills with sighs, ghosts.

The faculty retreat is over. We place our agendas into the ceremonial brazier, and as they burn, we forget. Where are we? Who?

Who?

Nine of Swords

Adrienne is lying in the nurse's office because she told Mr. Jackson she was going to barf, and Mr. Jackson will believe anyone who says they're sick. Supposedly he didn't one time and ended up with a ruined sport coat.

She's not actually sick. Mostly she needed to escape. Twenty minutes from now, when second period ends, Jasper will discover what she slipped through the vent in his locker. It's a page she ripped out of Tara's journal, at Tara's house, when Tara was in the bathroom. Tara had shoved the journal under her mattress, and later said something disparaging about Adrienne's clothes, so as soon as Tara left the room, Adrienne opened the journal and struck gold: a six-paragraph sex fantasy about Jasper Imhof.

That day, Adrienne was wearing a plaid pearl-snap shirt, dark jeans, cowboy boots, and a leather belt with hand-tooled rosettes. Tara said she looked like a hick. Adrienne *is* a hick. She wants to move back to Wyoming to live with her dad. But Mom got custody and they live in Denver with Hank, a medical-equipment salesman. Today, Adrienne is wearing a floral-print pearl-snap shirt, dark jeans, cowboy boots, and a leather belt with hand-tooled mountains. She figured if she wrecked her life, she'd be sent away, sent back to Dad.

But now, lying on the cot, with the nurse filling out forms beside her, her eyes fall upon a poster of the fencing team, nine clean-cut kids in white, their foils in the air, and she can't remember the last time Dad called. Dread is creeping up through her body and she tastes bile. Maybe she really will barf.

It's going to work. Her life will soon be over, and then what?

The Museum of Near Misses

I was traveling through the American Midwest, around what I had reason to expect would be the midpoint of a grueling, months-long book tour, when I got a call from an old friend. "Acquaintance" is perhaps a more appropriate term, or "former friend," as I'd long since cut my ties to this person, having found him unreliable, manic in the extreme, and conspiracy minded: a crackpot, if you will. He told me that he'd heard I'd be giving a reading not far from a small town called Alder, and he wondered if I'd mind doing him a favor. "There's something there that I want," he told me: a painting that, six years before, he'd lost by a hair at an auction in New York— unfairly, he added, implying that some hidden machinations had favored his rival—and that now hung, his research indicated, in a small museum in the aforementioned village. My friend's calls and emails to the museum had gone unanswered, its website was down, and he suspected the place might be preparing to liquidate its collection. He wanted me to drive to the museum, find out if the painting was really there, and, if so, buy it for him.

At any other moment on my tour, and to any other favor, I would have said no. But I didn't know anyone in this part of the country and had six rainy hours to kill before my reading; and the alternative was to camp out in my motel room and watch television. I didn't intend to actually carry out the request—knowing my friend and his proclivities, I'd probably be stuck with the painting—but my sense of adventure prevailed. I agreed.

Alder was a tiny farming community half an hour's drive from where I was staying, a low place of wide streets and grim, blocky storefronts. As I pulled into the center of town in my rental car, the drizzle turned to a violent downpour; the wind tore maple leaves from the trees and they smacked my windshield like desperate hands. I tugged my jacket up over my head and made a run for it, finding shelter on the steps of the museum.

A filthy glass door proclaimed its name in gilt: THE MUSEUM OF NEAR MISSES. The place was imposing only in comparison with the buildings that surrounded it; perhaps it had been a grange hall once, or a seat of government. The structure, two stories high, was of stone; its linteled windows were covered from the inside. Its entrance was sheltered by the portico I now stood beneath, flanked by stone columns. I peered through the glass and into the murk; the place looked closed. Indeed, the entire municipality of Alder appeared abandoned; I wasn't even going to bother to try the door. I was startled, however, by the sudden appearance, mere inches from my face, of a pair of rheumy eyes peering out from beneath a peaked cap: the custodian of the place. The door flew open before me and he welcomed me in. He was an old man, retired, no doubt, from the feed store or tractor mechanic's office where he'd spent his life of labor. For a moment I failed to comprehend his outstretched hand; I had the strange, passing impulse to kiss it. But then I saw the sign behind him announcing the admission fee. Surprised, I paid it.

I might have preferred to tour the museum on my own, but the custodian guided me, his hard-soled shoes scuffing along the gray floor and his threadbare cardigan exuding the scent of naphthalene. Exhibits lay in shadow in cracked glass vitrines, their labels yellowed and peeling; when the custodian used his sleeve to wipe away years of dust, the glass rattled and groaned like a sick old woman roused from sleep. The exhibits were hyperbolic in claim, unimpressive in substance: a child's tricycle that had almost, but not quite, been swept away by a tornado. A brick, half-shattered by a bullet from a faulty rifle, an artifact of what nearly was, but ultimately wasn't, the accidental shooting of the mayor of Davenport. The taxidermied carcass of a house cat known to have slept every day on the sixth-floor fire escape of a St. Louis tenement without ever falling to its death.

We stopped before an unmarked bell jar containing an irregular dark mass—an ossified, fibrous object propped up by what appeared to be a pair of six-sided dice.

"What is it?" I demanded.

"Its exact composition remains unknown," the custodian croaked, obviously following a script in his head. "It is believed to be the issue of a certain quarter horse that was not quite bought from a local farmer at an astronomical price, by a Russian prince wishing to race it."

"But . . . the prince didn't buy the horse, you're saying."

"No, sir. The sale was not completed."

"This is the horse's . . . issue, you say."

"Its exact composition," the custodian repeated, "remains unknown, sir."

"You're telling me it's horseshit."

But the custodian had moved on, farther into the gloom. "And now I call your attention to this skull!" he cried, gesturing toward a desiccated object on a shelf.

I did not follow, however, because at that moment I spied, partly concealed by an ill-placed curtain, the very object I'd been sent here to find: a four-foot-tall portrait, rendered in acrylic, of disgraced real estate mogul and former presidential candidate Donald J. Trump.

In truth, I owed some measure of my success to Trump. When, in 2016, he lost the presidential election to Hillary Clinton, I was commissioned by an online magazine to write a speculative short story about the ill-fated candidate, one that imagined a world in which, implausibly, he had become president. The story proved unexpectedly popular, and served as a study for the novel that, two years later, propelled me out of the literary backwater I had long inhabited, and onto the best-seller list. My life had been transformed; I now wrote mostly sequels and traveled the world promoting them. It was, I suppose, the life I'd longed for, but now, standing before this unlikely portrait, I felt a deep sadness of uncertain cause.

Trump had largely been forgotten, in the wake of his arrest and death in prison. It's difficult to describe the heady extremes of those days immediately following the election; Trump's accusations of tampering, the riots, the fears of a violent populist uprising. But then the courts convicted him of fraud and sexual assault; and Russian *kompromat* surfaced that depicted a naked Trump performing sexual acts upon a bound and quite possibly unwilling girl. And then there was the mysterious fire and the suspected poisoning and the tax evasion, and the Trumpist movement faded, embarrassed, back into the flyover wilds of rural America, where I now stood, gazing for the first time in years at the face I had once hated with such passion. This painting was famous, in its way; a campaign imbroglio had arisen around the misappropriated funds used to commission it. But, in the end, the painting's provenance was merely a detail, lost in the tidal wave of evidence that had made Trump, it was clear in hindsight, utterly unelectable.

The custodian had noticed my absence and come to stand at my shoulder. "Sir, the tour."

"Tell me," I said. "How might I go about buying this painting?"

"The museum's collection, sir," the custodian replied in a wounded tone, "is not for sale."

But I pressed him, demanding the name of the museum's director, and where he might be found. A bit of cajoling and the old man folded; the director was a retired bank loan officer, a Mr. Virgil, who lived just a block away and was probably at home right now. I thanked the custodian, turned on my heel, and strode out the door.

The rain had stopped and the clouds had parted, revealing a sky of the deepest blue. Bright sun shone upon Alder's grim streets, lending them a freshness I knew was illusory and that would disappear the moment the rain dried up and the hour grew late. But for now I watched a young woman crossing the street in a floral dress and jean jacket, her sneakers splashing through the puddles. Headphone cables trailed from her ears and into her pocket. She turned to me and I smiled, and she gave me the finger.

Mr. Virgil's house was a tidy bungalow surrounded by a white picket fence. I passed through the gate and knocked on a heavy oaken door, which opened to reveal a small, rotund man with the round face, haloed in white hair and whiskers, of a Samoyed puppy. I pointlessly identified myself ("the writer J. Robert Lennon" appeared to mean nothing to him) and stated my intention to buy the portrait of Donald Trump.

I expected to have to bargain, but his answer surprised me. "I would be delighted to sell, Mr. Lennon," he said, "but I'm afraid there is no such picture in our museum."

"You're mistaken," I replied. "I have just seen it. *Portrait of Donald J. Trump*, by one Havi Schanz."

"No," the director said, stroking his beard, "there are no portraits in the Museum of Near Misses. What would be the point?"

I wanted to offer the rejoinder that there didn't seem to be much point to the museum itself—things failed to happen for good reasons, I would have argued, and there was no need to dwell on what might have been—but instead I repeated to him that I'd just seen the painting five minutes before. Mr. Virgil reiterated his denial that the painting existed. We both declaimed our honesty and sanity, and Mr. Virgil appeared confident that the topic had been settled. "I hope you enjoyed the museum!" he exclaimed. "Did you see the quarter horse issue?"

"Look, Virgil," I said, my voice breaking. "Come to the museum with me. If I am right, and the Trump is there, agree that you will sell it to me. And if it isn't . . . I will pay you the money anyway!"

Virgil registered surprise and amusement, and, after a moment's thought, produced a sheet of paper from a nearby inkjet printer. "Take this red-and-blue pencil, and, using the red—the red, please—put it in writing for me."

I did what he asked, albeit with a sinking feeling. Had the custodian phoned him while I was in the street, warning him of my approach? Had Virgil told the custodian to take the Trump down from

the wall and hide it away? I began to plot my escape from the agreement, even as I codified it with my hand, having impulsively flipped
the pencil around to the blue point.

Virgil didn't seem to notice. The agreement clearly delighted
him. He signed, too, using the red end of the pencil, and stood up,
motioning me to join him. We strode out the door together, and I
followed him across the street, first to the gas station next door to the
museum, where Virgil bought himself a can of soda and a package of
Red Vines. He sipped hungrily from the former, then gestured to me
with the can. "Pepsi?" he offered, with a wink. I declined.

The museum had been transformed in our absence. A school
bus was parked on the street outside, and the dusty halls were filled
with rowdy young men dressed in dirty padded uniforms—a football team, on its way back from a game. Their loud voices echoed
in the dusty spaces; every now and then a stooped, vexed-looking
man, doubtless their coach, blew ineffectually into a whistle that
hung from his neck. One of the young men cawed and flapped his
arms, in imitation of a stuffed crow behind glass; another stuck out
his behind in front of the horse dropping and grunted, as though he
himself were extruding it.

Virgil and I, however, were undaunted; I think he was as eager
to prove his point as I was to prove mine. I led him to the spot where
the painting was displayed; to my relief, it was still there. Virgil stared
at it for several long seconds.

"Well, friend," he said, "I stand corrected!" And he tore up, with
evident glee, our signed agreement.

"Shall we settle on a price, then?" I inquired, still debating, privately, whether to spend an exorbitant amount of my eccentric
friend's money to punish him for his presumption, or to bargain
Virgil down as far as possible, as a hedge against the real possibility
that I might never be reimbursed.

But "Follow me!" the little man exclaimed, and he hurried off
into the darkness, where a dim red EXIT sign glowed. He moved
nimbly and swiftly, and I had to jog to catch up. At one point we
pivoted to avoid two football players arranged in a skillful imitation

of a nearby bronze statue: that of Muhammad Ali dodging Michael Dokes's frantic barrage of punches in their famous 1977 bout.

Over his shoulder, Virgil said to me, with a wink, "These young men! Aren't their uniforms snazzy?"

"Mr. Virgil!" I said, winded. "Aren't we going to discuss the sale?" We were passing through a dimly lit room containing mannequins, all male, displaying the accoutrements of soldiers, and, among them, tables piled high with discarded fashion magazines. OUR DAPPER NEW LEADERS! screamed a headline.

"Patience, Mr. Lennon!" he called back cheerfully. "The museum's treasures are also Alder's treasures, and the mayor must approve all sales! At the moment she's on a hiking trip, and has been for some time."

"But . . . when do you expect her back?" I cried, as we passed through another dim hall, this one empty save for a motley collection of baseball caps bearing an illegible message, hanging on pegs from the walls. I slowed to get a closer look, but an illustrated sign caught my eye instead. At first it appeared to be the same choking-response poster that hangs in every restaurant in the state of New York, but, upon closer examination, it clearly depicted a man in a suit grabbing a woman by the crotch. HOW TO WIN, the legend read.

"Back?" Virgil shouted, with a little laugh. I could barely see him now, through the gloom of the next hall, which seemed to feature a winter scene, complete with artificial-snow-covered trees, low-hanging cotton clouds suspended by wires, and a papier-mâché newsboy, holding up a newspaper whose headline blared THE CLIMATE CHANGE HOAX. "There's no telling when she'll be back, if at all! But don't worry, Mr. Lennon, you'll get your Trump!"

I couldn't see Virgil at all anymore, could only hear his footsteps receding into the distance. How could the little man move so fast? I doubled over, panting. The hall I found myself in was silent and almost completely dark, save for a large object looming deep in the murk, something blue and white and bulbous, like the nose cone of a huge bomb. After a moment, I laughed at my misapprehension: it was not a bomb, but an aircraft, a jet. On its flank the letters UNITED STA . . . faded into darkness, and a stairway descended from an open door, where a figure emerged in a smoky blaze of ochre . . .

I sensed more than saw a light in the distance, away from the plane, and I moved toward it, anticipating liberation from the absurdities of the museum and from my friend's ill-fated mission. Cold air met my face and I breathed it in . . . something bracing and dank, urban, with rank notes of subway and the toasted flavors of nuts and salted pretzels. The light intensified, turned golden, and I could make out, not just a door, but a magnificent wall of windows, latticed in gold. Beyond them people moved to and fro in heavy coats, and traffic passed; I knew I had found the exit from the museum and would soon be sitting in my car, listening to the radio and rehearsing the introduction to my reading. "Thank you all for coming," I would say. "Delighted to see you here this evening. No . . . *overjoyed* to see you here. This is so gratifying. No, such an *honor*. An honor to bask with you, on this rainy night, in our shared love . . . of story." To hell with Virgil, and the painting, and my friend, and the mayor lost forever in the woods. The real world beckoned.

Perhaps I could have turned back—retraced my steps, found my way past the jet and the statue and the horseshit and the custodian, and returned to the world from which I'd come. But I don't think so. I think my fate had been sealed when I beheld the painting, or when I answered my former friend's call, or earlier still, when I elected to live a life of self-deception, a life dictated not by reality but by the seductive and shapely contours of fiction.

In any event, I was through the lobby and out the revolving door before I realized what had happened, before the falling snow told me that it was no longer autumn but winter, late January, to be precise, and the noise of traffic and the blaze of yellow cabs told me I was not in the village of Alder but in the place where my imagination had resided for so many years, the place that, I now understood—even before the Secret Service agents threw me to the ground, their radios crackling—I would never be allowed to leave.

I don't have to describe that place to you. You have always lived there. I caught a horrifying glimpse of it before my face hit the pavement: the scrum of sign-bearing protesters, half decrying the family that, it was now clear, would not be dislodged from office without armed revolution; the other half demanding the imprisonment of the intellectuals and the gays, the silencing of the Blacks and the Jews, the expulsion of the Mexicans, the extermination of the Muslims. I heard them cheering on the agents as they lunged at me, tasers ablaze. I caught a glimpse of a sign on the other side of Fifth Avenue—PRADA, it read—and, underneath, its groomed and moneyed patrons calmly gliding to and fro behind another gilded glass facade, the exchange of goods and money proceeding without interruption, as though there were nothing in the world less remarkable than a random man emerging from the president's tower and being brutally subdued by police. Because there wasn't. Such things happened every day and were relevant to no one.

But enough. I'll spare you the story of my imprisonment and subsequent ordeals, which pale in comparison to the struggles of others, many of whose lives ended violently. Perhaps mine will, too, when all is said and done. All I can tell you today is that none of this is my fault. I'm not from here. Where I'm from, we clearly did something right, but I'll be damned if I know what it is.

The Cottage on the Hill (III)

It was twenty years before he returned to the cottage on the hill. His children had grown and moved away, and his ex-wife was dead. He had once hoped to remarry, but never did. In the end, Richard was satisfied with his solitude and didn't wish to disrupt it.

A business trip was to bring him across the state, and he realized that he would have to pass near the cottage. He still recalled, with real affection, that first visit, and the sense of hope that had lodged in him then; there was some part of him that believed he might have saved his family, perhaps even his wife's life, had he tried a little harder. In the intervening years, Lila had entered into therapy, where terrible ideas about him had been put into her head; she accused him, humiliated him at an extended-family gathering, even threatened to take legal action against him. Greg no longer spoke to him, either, having sided with his sister; in any event he had joined the military, grown a bushy mustache, and adopted a gruff, threatening manner.

And so it was with mixed feelings, curiosity strongest among them, that Richard pulled up to the site of the former substation. He peered out the window at the hillside he was certain must be the right one, but which nevertheless looked entirely alien. High-tension wires now ran overhead, supported by a massive steel tower, its enormous feet planted in the rocky soil. The trailer/office was gone, a cracked concrete slab in its place; the only definitive landmark was the cluster of rusted pipes that jutted from the weedy ground.

Richard got out of his car and climbed, effortfully, up the hill, feeling the hum of the power lines deep in his body. He was older now, and the hill more rugged, so by the time he reached the top he was winded, and his joints throbbed with pain.

The oak tree was gone, a rotting stump the only evidence that it had once existed. But the real differences lay with the cottage and the view. The far side of the hill had undergone a shocking transformation—half of it seemed to be missing, dug up and carted away. The gentle slope that had once led to the lake, and later the marsh, was now a cliff, its face revealing the gray of sediment and the red of clay. Below, the marsh was gone too. Now a thin, meandering creek ran through the valley, looking poisoned, a twist of bare wire.

The cottage stood in its usual place, but it had been half-undermined by the excavation. Someone must have wanted to preserve the old place, though, because the foundation had been extended down the cliffside in the form of a fifty-foot cinder block wall. Richard felt vertigo just looking at it.

But he had come this far. The cottage itself looked sturdy enough—in fact, its wooden walls and framing had been replaced by more cinder blocks, these painted a glossier, darker version of their natural gray. The windows had been eliminated, presumably to keep out the elements, and the once-sloping shingled roof was now little more than an angled sheet of corrugated metal.

Richard stepped carefully over some trash on the ground—an old doll, a box of books, some pieces of clothing, tangled in the weeds—and approached the cottage door. Beside it, a rusted hatchet was half buried in the oak stump, the surface of which appeared stained. Perhaps chickens had been raised and slaughtered here. The door, which he remembered as hardwood, with panes of glass, was now hollow-core steel, and stood halfway open, creaking quietly in the wind.

He was disappointed to find the cottage almost entirely empty. Indeed, the interior walls had been demolished, the floorboards torn up and replaced with concrete. The cottage was more like a garage now, or a warehouse. It smelled of earth and air.

As his eyes adjusted to the dark, Richard was able to make out only two objects in the room. A mattress lay in one corner. It was thin and pinstriped and appeared clean. And in the opposite corner stood a chair, a threadbare recliner, its upholstery rotting off and its stuffing removed, perhaps by mice. An old gray blanket lay curled on it, almost in the form of a sleeping person.

The longer he stood there, staring, the more Richard became convinced that there *was* a person sitting there, in the chair—that the blanket was actually a tiny woman in a gray dress, lying with her head resting against the chair's wing. When he gazed directly at the chair, the shape appeared to be a blanket, but in his peripheral vision, when he looked away, it again became a woman. Similarly, the mattress now seemed to bear the weight of a small child of indeterminate gender, pressed into the corner—he could almost make out its shape in the gloom. The child, like the woman, disappeared upon closer examination. Only if he stared straight ahead, into the far wall, could he discern both the woman and child at once.

He stood this way for some time. Outside, rain began to fall. Wind whistled through the open door behind him, and several times he thought he heard someone speak a name. Was it the old woman who had spoken? The child? Or was it someone else?

FOUR

Breadman

Of course I'd seen them, his customers, walking past the diner and thrift shop and firehouse clutching their oil-stained kraft paper sacks—disheveled and outdoorsy, these white Americans, healthy looking in an unpremeditated way, skin unblemished and tanned, muscles toned. You wouldn't catch them doing sports, but you might see a pair of them walking down the shoulder of a county highway in big floppy hats; you might encounter a bunch out in the woods in summer, casually fording a stream in technical sandals. They had money, which they appeared rarely to spend. Their glasses were likely to have hinged clip-on sunshades attached; the books in their satchels came from the public library. These people had no name—though they were many in our town, they didn't self-identify; the idea would have seemed silly to them. But the Breadman brought them together in this working-class neighborhood every Friday morning. It was the only way to get the bread—or, as my wife liked to call it, The Bread. You had to come here, to this little tchotchke shop that shared an entrance with the children's used-clothing store, where the Breadman set up his table, at precisely ten thirty in the morning—or, rather, half an hour before that, if you wanted The Focaccia, which couldn't be reserved, and was bestowed only upon the prompt. But I'm getting ahead of myself. I wouldn't have come here on my own in a million billion years. I liked the bread, but not that much. My wife sent me. She had a cold. That's why this happened.

Of course I was late. Which is to say, ten minutes early. There were thirty people ahead of me in line—men and women, but mostly women. Young to middle-aged, but mostly middle-aged. I am middle-aged. But the Breadman's People had the comfortable, self-possessed air of travelers from some great distance, who had at last arrived at their ultimate destination.

They chatted amiably and unostentatiously, smiled and laughed. None of them looked at their phones. I did, because I was by myself, and because I lived most of my life at a distance from the things and people I loved. It was also a quality of mine that I invariably became the terminus of any queue I joined. I took a photo of the people ahead of me and uploaded it onto the internet, along with the caption "Standing in the bread line! What is this, Soviet Russia?" A couple of minutes later, I deleted it.

Pretty soon the Breadman arrived with his assistants. I'm trying to say that without particular emphasis, because I don't like the Breadman and want to downplay his star power. But it was quite an entrance. He pulled up to the curb in a red boxlike van that resembled an oven, to gentle applause from the customers. The panel door rolled open and a couple of stringy, deeply tanned kids in their twenties hopped out, a boy and a girl, and unloaded the Breadman's gear wearing serious expressions. A folding table, a cash box, a stool; several large hinged wicker crates containing the bread; a freestanding painted wood sign that read *Manna* in a bubbly but somehow pedantic script, and then underneath, in precise all-caps sans-serif, QUALITY BREADS. The kids made two trips into the tchotchke shop before the Breadman emerged, and when he did, ambling around the snout of the van while distractedly riffling through pages fixed to a clipboard, a chorus of greetings went up from the crowd.

"Anton! Anton!"

The Breadman looked up as though surprised. He smiled, gave everyone a little wave. "Hello, everybody! Thank you for coming. We'll be set up in just a moment."

He was my age, which is to say midforties, but much better looking and much more at ease in his own skin. That skin was white,
of course, which is not to say pale; it was as though he had been
brushed with egg white and baked to an even brown. He wore large
eyeglasses with black plastic frames over vaguely Semitic, bookish
features, and his black hair and beard were flecked with gray. The
gray made him more handsome. His short-sleeved silk shirt was also
black, and dusted with flour, as were his tailored jeans. The flour
seemed a bit theatrical to me—yes, he was a baker, but were these
really the clothes he baked in? I suspected it had been added inten-
tionally, as a marker of artisanal legitimacy. His feet were bare.

It was unclear to me why the tchotchke shop had been chosen as
the pickup point. It was situated far from where his customers were
likely to live, in a neighborhood that, while quite safe by city stan-
dards, was nevertheless the staging ground for most of our town's
violent crimes. For that matter, I didn't know why the tchotchke
shop had chosen this location in the first place—I never saw any-
body there. It seemed to be some kind of craftspeople's collective,
though all the merchandise looked the same—faux-primitive rep-
resentations of semirural small-town life, rendered on coffee mugs,
greeting cards, T-shirts, and, in what could be seen only as a deliberate effort to deter potential buyers, mouse pads. In any event, all
of this was now pushed aside to accommodate the ingress of the
Breadman's customers. Since I was the last, I spent the first ten minutes of the selling period in the unventilated glass vestibule, endur-
ing the magnified summer heat.

I texted my wife: *doors open.*

don't forget the focaccia, she texted back.

that's a kind of coffee right, I replied.

pls just get it.

Looking at that exchange now—I have never deleted a text—
I can see that trust was the issue. She didn't trust me and never had.
Which is not to say that I blame anyone but myself for what was to
happen. I was sweating: marshy pits, swamp ass. The women who
had been first in line now edged past me on their way out, keeping as

great a distance between us as they could in the elevator-sized space, assisted by their giant paper sacks of The Bread, The Focaccia poking out of the top.

Chuckles and smiles. "Pardon me."

"Pardon *me*!"

The line accordioned; I entered the tchotchke shop. I picked up, fondled, a coffee mug made to resemble a terra-cotta flowerpot. TEN SQUARE MILES OF HAPPY! read its bold text, superimposed on the outline of our county. To an outsider, the outline wouldn't look like anything much at all: a chip of old latex paint, a torn postage stamp. But an outsider would never buy this mug, except ironically.

Now that I was inside, the air-conditioning cooled the sweat patches on my clothes, and I began to shiver. Luckily there was coffee here, at the front of the line. It came from the coffee shop down the block, and was contained within a mailbox-sized waxed cardboard tote. A stack of paper cups stood beside it; an aluminum honor box bore a sticky note reading $1. Next to that lay an important thing that I had forgotten about: the clipboard. If you wanted The Bread, you had to sign in—specifically, to write your last name and first initial on a neatly hand-ruled table (*Print clearly*, warned a note at the top). Then you added your signature. Then you had to write your account number. My wife had explained this process to me, and we had rehearsed it together.

"Five, one, zero, nine, three," I had said.

"Say it again. Five, one, zero, nine, three."

"Five, one, zero, nine, three."

"Just write it down. You're going to forget it."

"Five, one, zero, nine, three," I said. "I don't need to write it down! Five, one, zero, nine, three."

Of course I remember it now, but I didn't remember it then. I texted her, *account number?*, and then, after a moment's thought, added, *:) <3*. That done, I left my place in line to pour myself a coffee and check in. The Breadman's People glared at me as I passed. Why? I was obeying the rules!

All I had was a five, so I dropped it into the honor box and withdrew three singles. The extra dollar was a tip. Anton was standing six feet to my left, lecturing a zaftig blond woman about spelt. He glanced coolly in my direction at the clank of the honor box lid, but didn't pause in his patter.

I held up the three singles, mouthed the word *change*, and winked.

As I helped myself to the coffee, my wife's text came in. *51093*, it read. I dutifully copied this onto the appropriate line, along with my wife's name and initial, and her forged signature. I hazarded another look at the text message. Could a five-digit number read as hostile? Yes, it could. I should call my wife something other than "my wife." Let's go with "Kathy," since that is her real name.

The Breadman was saying, "It is among the most ancient of grains. At one time it was plentiful in Europe and the Near East, but now it is a relic*t* crop." He really leaned on that *t*. I had to look this up later—it's a word. "Relict," with a *t* at the end. He said it again. "A relic*t*, though some of us have had success reviving its use in certain enlightened communities. It is also valued as a brewer's grain."

"Fascinating," said the blond woman.

"How many focaccia would you like, Angela? One or two?"

"Two, please."

When I returned to the back of the line with my coffee, I discovered that a man had taken my place. He was around seventy years of age and wore a long white beard and ponytail, each kept in place by a hair scrunchie. He held a bicycle helmet. I considered asking to reoccupy my rightful station, but I reasoned that it didn't matter. I had signed in before him. I wedged myself between him and the door and dispassionately slurped my coffee.

The old man made no move toward the clipboard, so I said, "You gotta sign in."

He didn't seem to hear me. He gazed out the window, at the slow-moving people and cars.

"Hey. Sir."

He turned.

"You gonna sign in?" I said. "Pretty sure you have to sign in."

The man's placid, wordless smile served as a dismissal, and he returned to his window-gazing.

Fine.

No one else entered behind me as the line slowly diminished. I was not frustrated by the wait: I had my coffee, I had signed in, and I needed only to anticipate receiving the Breadman's bounty. I didn't even feel compelled to look at my phone. This mode of being is something that Kathy referred to, rather unimaginatively, as "smug mode." "You just stand there," she said, "with this incredible air of self-satisfaction, as though all is right in the world and you are majestically enthroned at the center of it." This characterization was both apt and extremely flattering; I gather the latter was not her intention.

It occurred to me, as I observed the Breadman's languorous, deliberate servicing of his customers, accompanied by the energetic, even frantic, unsmiling efforts of the assistants (removing bread from the baskets, inserting bread into sacks, making change), that the entire operation had been designed first and foremost not as a baked-goods distribution scheme but as a formalized, even ceremonial, vehicle for the expansion and annealment of Anton's self-regard. Every aspect of it was obscure. It was a laboratory maze for the Breadman's People, a test of their devotion, and a method of schooling them in the proper rituals. The odd location; the inconvenient time (one that precluded the participation of anyone with a nine-to-five job); the complex, redundant paperwork; the strategic withholding of the one thing everyone wanted: The Focaccia.

But I haven't adequately described The Focaccia. It presented not as a conventional flatbread but as a twelve-inch-diameter half round, three inches high at the center, tapering to an inch at the edges. Its crust was faintly lambent, aglow with some ineffable crispy glaze, which harbored visibly intact crystals of sea salt and an evidently proprietary blend of coarsely chopped herbs that certainly included rosemary and dill, among less immediately identifiable vegetative bits. The flesh within was richly grained, chewy, and very moist—

oily, even—which gave the bread a deep yellow-brown color when toasted. It was not necessary to butter it—it was so rich—but you would have been a fool not to.

The Focaccia's crust was crisscrossed by a series of seemingly random slashes that nevertheless intersected in a complex, snowflake-like pattern. It wasn't until some time later, while walking to an appointment with the woman who prescribed my antidepressants, that I passed a young man wearing a T-shirt bearing the anarchy symbol—the slashed letter *A* inside a rough circle—and realized that the pattern on The Focaccia had been composed of the letters *A* and *V*, artfully reiterated: *A* and *V*, as in Anton Vainberg, the Breadman's full name. I literally jumped as I realized it, startling the punk rocker who'd prompted the revelation, and told my pharmacologist as soon as I entered the office. But she merely nodded, suggested I save it for my therapist, and cut my dosage, as she had warned me she had been planning to do.

Back in the bread line, I did my best to enjoy my coffee and smug mode, as I listened to the Breadman's patter with his disciples—gratuitous inquiries into their personal lives, and into the lives of their adult children and pets. "Where's Boomer today?" "How's little Pete?" If the follower was a woman alone, the Breadman always asked after the husband or wife or partner, as though to say, "Now, now—I know you want to fuck me, but think of your significant other. How will he or she feel when our affair is discovered?"

Of course, what everyone really wanted was The Focaccia, two loaves for most. The Focaccia lived in its own special basket, a four-foot rattan cylinder the assistants had to keep leaning farther and farther into, as though into a magic hat for a series of rare and desirable rabbits. I had lost hope—surely it would be gone before I reached the table.

I wasn't last in line, though—the old man was. I had to admit to myself, even inside the protective force field of smug mode, that this disparity—between the old man's rightful and actual positions in line—had begun to bother me. And it bothered me more and more as the line diminished. With only a few people remaining, and the

Breadman beginning to repeat his monologue about baking times and temperatures, about the burning qualities of various woods and the medicinal properties of certain seeds, I was ejected from smug mode entirely, and began to huff and puff and steal glances at my phone. One of the two assistants, the boy, clapped the dust off his hands and walked around behind me to the door, which he locked, presumably to prevent the entry of newcomers. He remained stationed there as a reverse-jailer, to allow each customer out once he or she had accepted the Breadman's largesse. As the last middle-aged couple departed, the boy assistant produced a tight smile that was gone by the time he locked the rest of us back in.

The old man stood at the front of the line now—it was just him, me, and the Manna crew. "Anton," he said, his voice a dried strap of leather.

The Breadman's entire demeanor changed. His shoulders sloped, the haughtiness vanished from his face. He held both hands out, palms up, and the old man took them into his own.

"Spokefather," the Breadman said, penitent and husky. He released the man's hands, came around the buffet table, and enveloped him in a brief embrace. The two kissed each other's cheeks.

The assistants, as though broken from a spell by the Breadman's affection, approached the old man, bowed slightly, and uttered the word that I now understood to be his name.

"Spokefather."

"Spokefather."

Conversation was lively, obsequious. The Manna crew inquired about the old man's "European sojourn," and his "spiritual quest," which may or may not have been the same thing. They asked after "Old Bones," who I gathered was some kind of ailing animal companion.

"Friends," the old man said, "how do you roll?"

"Well, Spokefather. We roll well."

And now the old man asked the questions. Anton's sister: how rolled she? The assistants, did their child thrive? (I hadn't pegged them as breeders, those two.)

She rolls well, Spokefather. Spokefather, the child is strong.

For my own part, I felt entirely invisible. These four were locked in some kind of devotional symbiosis—an energy similar to, but more powerful than, that which the Breadman enjoyed with his subjects. Indeed, I wondered if I was observing the spiritual antecedent of the Breadman's fellowship, the original to which it aspired.

I briefly forgot why we were all there. Then, with a deep, satisfied sigh, Anton turned to his friend and god, and said, "Spokefather, what may I offer you today?"

"Two focaccia, friend."

"Excellent," said the Breadman, and he bent over the basket, personally withdrew the last two loaves, and slid them carefully into a paper sack while the girl assistant snatched up the empty vessel and spirited it away.

It took me a moment to absorb what was happening, which left me with little time to compose my objection. Not that more time would necessarily have improved it. I am rhetorically limited even in the most relaxed of circumstances. "Now, wait a minute," I said.

All heads snapped up. They were clearly surprised to be reminded of my existence.

"I'm here specifically to buy my wife—my sick wife—some of that focaccia," I said. "And I was here before this gentleman, and he never signed in."

They stared.

"So those loaves," I continued, borrowing a phrase from myself, "are rightfully mine to buy."

No response.

"Are they not?" I added.

The assistants exchanged alarmed glances. The old man appeared beatific—on his face a faint smile appeared, and his eyes fell shut. He tipped his head back slightly, as though in anticipation of instructions from outer space. But he didn't speak.

Instead it was the Breadman who spoke. He said, "Aren't you Kathy's?"

The phrase was like a jolt—an electric shock to my neck and scalp.

I must have jerked slightly. I raised my hand to rub the affected area, trying to pass it off as a casual hair-smoothing.

"I am married to Kathy, yes," I said. "She asked me to pick up some focaccia." I pointed at my pocket, which held my phone. That's where Kathy lived, on my phone.

The Breadman nodded, not at what I'd said, it seemed, but at some unfathomably complex skein of interlocking events and personalities of which I was, could only ever be, dimly, inadequately aware. He trained a pitiful look upon me.

He said, "Kathy would understand."

Before I had a chance to digest this extraordinary remark, the male assistant stepped up beside me, threateningly close. His face was flushed and slick and he smelled of sweat and woodsmoke. He said, "The Focaccia are for Old Bones." Then he withdrew to the sidelines, where the other assistant waited with a comforting half hug and whispered reassurances.

"A dog?" I said.

"Old Bones is Spokefather's trusted friend," the Breadman explained. "He's in his last days now. The Focaccia are his favorite treat."

I turned to the old man, hoping for some kind of clarification. Surely he wasn't going to go along with this nonsense? But he was still examining the heavens through the insides of his eyelids and could not be reached.

"You have a system," I said. "That's my understanding. It is very elaborate and highly specific. What's the point of having a system if somebody can just walk in here, cut in line, and circumvent it? I signed the sheet. I marked my time!"

The boy assistant snorted and shook his head. The Breadman held out a calming hand, nodded, then pressed his fingertips together. He leaned forward, slightly.

"But this is Spokefather," he said.

"I'm sorry," I replied. "With all due respect, I don't know who the hell that is. I mean, yes, it's this guy, but isn't this a business? Isn't this a public-facing small business? Aren't I a customer? Aren't you in the business of selling bread?"

"We don't think of it that way," the girl assistant hissed.

"It's all right," the Breadman said now. "It's fine. We forgive you for this misunderstanding. But the fact is, you're here as an agent of Kathy, and Kathy will understand when you tell her that The Focaccia went to Spokefather and Old Bones. And her original order," he went on, "is right here." He gestured at the greasy sack standing on the table beside him. "One semolina ciabatta, a seeded eight-grain round, and six cracked-maize dinner rolls. You'll have all the bread you want. Kathy," he repeated, "will understand."

I should have just taken the bag and paid. But instead I said—shouted, I suppose—"What the hell do you know about Kathy?"

A silence ensued. The boy assistant's muscles tensed.

"We know Kathy very well. We've heard about you, too, Samuel. We are friends to your marriage, and to your bodily and spiritual well-being."

"The fuck?" was my response.

"We—all of us—love you, friend."

I don't want to give the impression that I regret my actions, because I do not. These events would prove to be the beginning of a long quest for self-knowledge and self-improvement that continues to this day. I am happier now, back in the city of my origin, with a calmer job and an earnest hope for a more suitable romantic partner, whom I expect to find once I have completed my transformation. No, "completed" is the wrong word: reached, let us say, the next level of my enlightenment. My only wish is that I had spent a few additional seconds plotting my next move, so that I might have enjoyed some small strategic advantage over the Breadman. Instead, I allowed my impulses to rule, and I did what the man expected—I drew my arm back and swung.

The boy assistant lunged for me, but it wasn't necessary: before I had completed my swing, the man they called Spokefather had knocked my feet out from under me with one sweep of his bony ankle, and I pitched helplessly over, driving my face into the corner of the buffet table before arriving at last on the floor. The doctors later told me that there must have been a loose bit of metal trim on there, because something thin and sharp had sheared a large flap of skin nearly off of my cheek. That's where all the blood came out. They had to guess, because I declined to tell them what had happened; the police were never summoned, and Kathy's insurance paid for the emergency treatment. I was later surprised to receive a cleaner's bill from the tchotchke shop—the nerve!—but, ultimately, I mastered my fury and paid it.

I never did go home. Lying there in the hospital bed, pressing the ice pack to my face, I took stock of everything I had observed and put it all together: the sandals, the unbleached fabrics, the unshaven legs and underarms. The rosy skin and weight gain and interest in watercolor painting. The jars filled with dried legumes. Soaps with food in them and food with flowers in it. Kathy was Breadman People. She had been for quite a while. She had taken a lover months before (no, not Anton—another of his followers) and had just been waiting—her letter on recycled paper eventually told me—for me to notice. My unwillingness to do so merely reinforced her confidence that she was in the right.

She was. I am not, have never been, a cad, but I was a terrible husband. Kathy would have been a fine wife for the appropriate man. Perhaps she is now. I don't know. I didn't reply to the letter. Our divorce was amicable and swift and conducted through intermediaries.

Of course I didn't learn to bake. Why would I do that? I hate those people and everything they represent.

Of course I can still eat bread. I'm not a child.

Of course I'm not happy. Are you?

Well, good for you, then.

Sympathy

She is in the stationery store to buy her daughter a birthday card, as she does every year, and happens across the section marked SYMPATHY. "In Memory of Your Loving Mother," reads one, in a tasteful script, and she wonders why it suddenly hurts her so badly: the pain of her own mother's death, years before, feels immediate and real. Of course it isn't the pain of losing her mother she is feeling, but the pain of losing her daughter, who has recently died of a brief illness. She has come here out of deeply ingrained habit. Nevertheless she buys her daughter a birthday card, one with a cartoon monkey on it, then leaves it in the glove compartment when she gets home from the mall.

Storm

He was texting somebody from bed. Trying to hide it from her—it wasn't clear who it was. Someone he shouldn't have been texting. The storm outside had woken him and now he was texting, and the lightning lit the room. The phone's LED flashed as he typed, and the sky answered, and the phone trembled in his hands. Now it spoke to the storm directly—it spoke in flashes, and the storm spoke back. It did not respond to his touch. Lightning struck—through the window, into the bed—and the phone tumbled from his hands. He had to find it. He tore through the bedclothes, gasping, the smell of ozone heavy and close. Where was it?

It was gone. The storm had taken it.

She was gone too. She'd taken everything when she left, even her pillow.

Notebook

Which is where she should have thought to look for the notebook: beneath the radiator she had set it down upon when the phone rang. After she observed, returning to the room, that he had come home, and was sitting on the sofa, and that the notebook was missing. Thus prompting her to say, "Well, now you know the truth. So are you staying or leaving?" While simultaneously noticing the corner of the notebook poking out from under the radiator it had fallen behind. The notebook between whose pages was folded the letter she had just told her friend, on the phone, that she had decided to burn instead of give to him. And which she later did burn, after his departure, when it no longer mattered.

Falling Down the Stairs

Falling down the stairs, he thinks: I'm falling down the stairs. He'll get where he was headed, and sooner than anticipated. But he won't be able to get his hands out fast enough to break his fall. He was carrying a tray of cupcakes, and his mind privileged the cupcakes over his physical well-being. That was a mistake. The cupcakes are for his daughter's birthday party. They're iced in pastels and sprinkled with coarse dyed sugar. There are two dozen cupcakes. They're hanging in the air before him, lifting off the dropped tray, abandoning the tight pattern he arranged them in, back on the kitchen counter.

The girls at the party haven't noticed him yet. They're seated around the buffet table wearing party hats, animatedly chatting. He was anxious earlier when one of them, the one named Hannah, was delivered by her father. That's because he loves Hannah's mother. Hannah's mother loves him. They've been having an affair—meeting once or twice a week at a motel. He wants to leave his wife—that is, his daughter's mother—and go live with his lover—that is, Hannah's mother.

Instead, he's falling down the stairs. He's halfway to the bottom now. A little table is standing there, at the bottom, a hardwood table he built himself. It supports a framed family photo: himself, his wife, and their daughter. He's going to hit the table with his face. The cupcakes are tumbling, drifting apart. One has struck the wall over the handrail, leaving a pink smear of icing on the brown plaid carpet that lines the rec room. Another cupcake is headed for the framed photo. Of the twenty-four cupcakes, two were intended for Hannah.

Yesterday, he made love to Hannah's mother in the motel bed. Today, his wife asked him to carry the cupcakes down to the party. He's not doing that anymore. Now he is falling down the stairs and wondering what it will be like if Hannah's mother divorces Hannah's father, as promised, and he becomes Hannah's stepfather. Will his own daughter come over to visit Hannah, his stepdaughter? Will that be odd? It will, he thinks, as the table draws closer and the beginning of a shout escapes his lips and the girls' heads begin to turn. The cupcake heading for the framed photo has missed the framed photo by an inch. I wish, he thinks, that I wasn't falling down the stairs. He had planned to tell his wife about Hannah's mother tomorrow, after their daughter left for school. But now he's falling down the stairs and tomorrow he will probably be in the hospital. Everything will be ruined.

But no, he thinks, as the cupcakes crash into the floor and wall, and his smiling face and his wife's smiling face and their daughter's smiling face gaze up at him from the rapidly approaching photo, and the girls begin to scream—everything was already ruined. It was ruined long before he fell down the stairs. Everything is ruin, he thinks, even love. Especially love, he thinks, and the table hits his face.

Marriage (Marriage)

She said, We need to talk about our marriage.

He said, What is there to say?

That's what we need to talk about, she said.

He said, We need to talk about how there's nothing to say about our marriage?

No, she said, we need to talk about your unwillingness to address the problems in our marriage.

That's not a problem in our marriage, he said. That's a problem with me. What's wrong with our marriage?

She took out her notebook and recited a list of the problems.

Those are all just complaints about me, he said. I could do the same thing.

He then recited, from memory, a list of complaints about her.

I see what you mean, she said. But I'm unhappy in our marriage. Are you?

Unhappy? he said. Yes.

She said, So, should we end our marriage?

He hesitated, seeming to grow angry in the silence. Then he burst out, arms waving in the air, You see! This is why we can't talk about our marriage!

But we're unhappy! she said.

He said, We're not supposed to be happy!

She threw down her notebook and shouted, You're such an asshole!

That's more like it, he said, smiling. So are you.

After a moment, she smiled as well.

Marriage (Sick)

She's lying on the sofa. She says, I think I feel sick.

You think? he says. How can you *think* you feel sick? Either you feel sick or you don't feel sick.

I don't know if I feel sick, she says.

He says, You don't know if you *are* sick. But surely you know if you *feel* sick.

I feel something, she says. And I don't like it. But I don't know what it is.

Well, again, he says. How do you know you don't like it if you don't know what it is?

She says, Fine. It's a bodily unease. It's the vaguest hint of nausea, coupled with the faintest headache, which might be the result of my posture, or not getting enough sleep. Or it could be the first sign of illness. These sensations are unclear. They fade in and out of perception as the patterns of my thoughts and actions change. Okay?

Maybe it's all in your head, he says.

I just told you it isn't. I just told you it is in my body.

Well, he says, you think it's your body. But it could be that it's your mind planting ideas in your body.

In other words, she says, it's my fucking body.

If you were really sick, he says, you'd know it. Believe me. There's no mistaking it when it comes on.

I've been sick before, you idiot, she says.

Well, he says, remember what that was like. Are you feeling that now?

I might be.

He makes a face.

You make me sick, she says.

He says, Aha, that's a clever bit of rhetoric. But in truth—

She vomits. It lasts awhile. A minute, at least. She makes no apparent effort to move to the toilet or to contain the vomit to a small area.

She says, I'm sick.

You're sick, he says. He leaves the room and comes back with a wet washcloth, a roll of paper towels, and a bottle of spray cleaner. He cleans off her face and then the furniture and floor. He leaves the room and comes back with a cup of tea and a blanket. He sets the tea on the coffee table and covers her with the blanket.

I'm sorry, he says.

She says, Are you sure?

Yes.

Maybe you're feeling something but you don't know what it is. That's a real phenomenon, she says, weakly. Maybe you're saying you're sorry because it's socially appropriate, but you're feeling something very different. Something you are too dense to have bothered to examine. Maybe you are feeling nothing at all.

He says nothing.

You're *sorry*, she says, making quotation marks with her fingers.

After a while, he goes upstairs. After a while, she starts to cry.

Marriage (Mystery)

She says, You weren't like this when I married you.

Like what? he says.

This way, she says. Doing the things that hurt me.

I have always been this way, he says. The things that hurt you are part of my essential nature.

You hid them from me, she says.

Because, he says, I wanted you to marry me. You wouldn't have married me if you'd known.

Then our marriage is a lie, she says.

No, he says. Our marriage is a mystery.

Eleven

Eleven: the number of days until he'll see her again; the number of times he says her name into his pillow every night and again when he wakes; the number of letters in her full name, spread over four syllables, one three four three; the number of steps from his bedroom to the bathroom where he balls eleven kleenex in his fist, one by one, and sails them across the room and into the wastebasket, starting over at one if he misses, and in the morning his father asks who in the hell is using all the goddam kleenex, and his mother says shush, don't make him feel bad; eleven times he touches the light switch when he leaves the bathroom to return to bed, eleven seconds he counts before he can roll over in the bed, eleven scratches on his itchy ankle, eleven insertions of his finger into each nostril when he gets the urge to pick his nose. Eleven is his age, and hers, and when she asked him, during math, what was with the tapping, because he had been making himself tap his desk eleven times on each corner with a pencil every time he imagined reaching across the space between them and stroking the dark skin of her resting hand, he said, It's a project I'm working on; and instead of rolling her eyes and turning away as most girls would she looked straight at him and said, with the faintest hint of a smile, Well that has got to be some project; and before the teacher yelled at the two of them to stop talking— the two of them, reprimanded together!—he thought Oh God, why tomorrow? why does winter break begin tomorrow? because when they returned in January she would be twelve and the one thing that connected them, the one thing that is real to him, would be gone, and she would never speak to or smile at him again; she would be part of a new world, the world of twelve, which at this moment, as he lies in bed on the first dreadful night of Christmas vacation, seems as distant to him, as cold and imaginary, as the North Pole.

Rest Stop

I am sitting across a concrete picnic table from Roland at the rest stop on the shoulder of Route 75. The sky is hot and bright and the three trees near us are perfectly placed so as to cast no shade upon where we are sitting. Roland is eating a giant sandwich out of a clear plastic clamshell and I am picking apart an unsmoked cigarette I found lying on the floor of Sera's hospital room. Sera is going to live. Her mother is flying in from Arkansas. The hospital is on the other side of the highway and can be reached from here via an elevated walkway. Roland was drunk when I picked him up and he is slightly less drunk now. Roland is Sera's father. The cigarette is probably Sera's. It probably fell from her pocket or purse when they brought her in. I don't for sure know what brand Sera smokes because I don't smoke with Sera because I don't smoke, and she's supposed to have quit, so she hides them from me. It is possible that Sera has brain damage. I'm not sure, because they wouldn't tell me, because they didn't believe I was Sera's wife. They would tell only Roland, who was drunk, and now Roland won't tell me, because he doesn't want me to be Sera's wife. It's a roast beef sandwich, on weck. I blame Sera's mother for not being there for Sera. I blame Roland for being there in the wrong way. I blame myself for being there but doing nothing to help, then not being there. I blame Sera for not being able to be helped. The cigarette's constituent parts, laid out before me on the concrete table, tremble, then skip across the painted surface, then fly away in the wind. Roland finishes the sandwich and looks around for a trash can. There is one, but he doesn't get up. The wind seizes the plastic clamshell, tugs it from his hands, and carries it into the road, where a truck runs it over. Sera and I separated four months ago after she tried to end her life. She blamed me, so I left. Her new roommate called me today; he'd found the empty pill bottle. The nurses said I saved Sera's life, bringing her here. Roland looked at me like why would you do such a thing. The cigarette is gone now, separated from itself. My body's making sweat faster than the sun can evaporate it. Roland's phone rings. He doesn't move. I say Aren't you going to answer that and he says You don't understand me or my fucking daughter at all.

Owl

His son wouldn't take the garbage out to the barn, because there was a bat, the boy said, flapping around out there; so the father muttered an oath, cinched the bag shut, and crunched across to the gravel driveway and through the dusk-darkened open door, only to find that the boy was right, there *was* something out there—not a bat, he realized as the thing swooped over his head and came to rest on the seat of a disused bicycle leaning against the rear window—a small gray owl, its back to the gloom, flinging itself futilely and halfheartedly against the still faintly lambent glass. It's confused, he thought, confused and lost, so he set down the sack of trash and took the owl gently into his two hands, planning to release it through the open door, which he would have done immediately had the owl not dug its claws into his fingers and puffed itself up inside his cupped hands and said, in a high, strangled croak, I'm not lost or confused and I'm not an owl, I'm the part of your son you don't understand, and I beat myself against the glass not because I want to escape but because I want to know how it feels; and while this speech from the owl gave him pause, he walked the rest of the way across the barn to the door and freed the thing into the night air, because he didn't know what else to do and because it frightened him to have the creature in his hands; then he dropped the trash bag into the garbage can as planned and went back into the house to apologize to his son.

Husbands

Her husband is often away. This shouldn't bother her—she is of an independent cast of mind, and married a similar man—but since they married she has come to appreciate the idea of the husband more than she expected to. Or, rather, the emergence of her natural inclination to favor the husband—or, to favor husbandness—has surprised her. When her husband is away, she misses both her husband and husbandness itself.

She has befriended her neighbor, an easygoing man who hangs out with her husband when her husband is in town. She and this man eat meals together at the café down the street. The neighbor likes to socialize, so when she is invited to a party and her husband is away, she asks the neighbor to join her. A colleague once asked her, "Are you bringing your husband to my party?" and she replied, "No, I am bringing my party husband."

Her job allows her to work alone, and she does this at a coffee shop. There is a man who makes her coffee every morning. He fusses over the espresso machine, then slides her coffee in its small china cup onto a china plate. He pushes the plate toward her across the wooden counter and then places upon it, beside the demitasse, the shortbread cookie he knows she likes to eat while she works. He is a man who serves her every day, who smiles at her and knows what she wants, so he, too, is a kind of husband—a coffee husband.

Once, she was at a party with her party husband, and she saw the coffee husband. She introduced the two as husbands of hers, and both appeared confused and ill at ease. Once, she went to the coffee shop with her actual husband, and confessed to him that she regarded the barista as her coffee husband, and her husband said, "That guy?" It's true that the barista is not the kind of man she would choose as an actual husband, and this is what her husband was reacting to—the idea of this man as an actual husband. She tried to explain the difference between the types of husband, but her husband seemed disturbed by, or perhaps uninterested in, the subject, and she let it go.

When her husband is away, and they talk on the phone, she tries to avoid telling him that she misses him, because she is supposed to be tough and unsentimental, the way she was when they married. And she is. But sometimes when the husband has to leave town, they've been fighting; and when they part, he is the fight husband, and she feels, when they talk on the phone in the days and weeks that follow, that he is still the fight husband, even if their conflict has cooled, because he hasn't been around to behave otherwise. She wants to use words to banish the fight husband, to draw out her ideal husband, but she isn't sure how he would react. After all, he doesn't know which husband he is. He thinks he's just the one guy.

It is true that, to her, her husband is actually many husbands. When he's funny, he is the joke husband, and when he says something nice to her, he is the compliment husband. Once, they were having sex and she thought, I'm having sex with my sex husband, and she began to laugh, and his feelings were hurt, and the sex stopped. Her explanation did not help matters. He got out of bed and became the fight husband. She lingered afterward, regretting the entire situation, and she wondered, where is the sex husband, the one who came to bed? Is he still here, too small to see? Where does he go when she isn't having sex with him? And then there is the more disturbing question: where is the fight husband when her husband is the sex husband, or compliment husband, or joke husband? He's in there, somewhere, waiting to fight. She knows this isn't a productive way to think about her husband.

She goes to a party with her party husband, and is reminded by a friend that there is a type of pillow called a husband. She is a little drunk when she gets home, and she gets on the internet and orders one. A few days later, the package arrives. The deliveryman gets out of the truck, and it's the same man who always delivers things to her house: her package husband. The package husband is quite handsome and she has, at times, wondered about his potential as an actual husband. She has idly fantasized about, though not actually considered, seducing the package husband. It's a common fantasy, she guesses. The package husband doesn't wear a ring; probably he has had sex with some of the people he delivers packages to. The idea of undressing the package husband introduces the idea of the package husband as a kind of package. He is a package, and he would deliver himself to her, and she would open the package that is the package husband and then he would become a sex husband. There are not supposed to be multiple sex husbands. As she accepts the package, which is large, she thanks the package husband, who is also large—tall, anyway—and tries to banish the thought of accepting the package that is him.

The package husband says, "That's a big box."

"Don't I know it," she says.

"Need any help with that?" asks the package husband, and she replies "no" perhaps a little too quickly, and she awkwardly grabs the giant box and heaves it backward into the house, letting the screen door slam shut between the package husband and herself.

Once the package husband has driven away, she opens the box and takes out the husband pillow. It's corduroy. It's ugly. Its name is derived from its shape: it stands upright, a kind of sofa cushion with two upholstery arms that extend out from its base. It's chair-like, lacking only the seat and legs. One—a lady, presumably—is supposed to lean back into it the way one might lean back into one's husband, if one's husband weren't out of town. She drags the husband pillow into the bedroom and heaves it up onto the bed, and then leans back into it and watches sitcom episodes on her laptop computer for two hours. The sitcoms, she notices, all involve husbands. These husbands are often difficult to get along with. They have often eaten something they were not supposed to eat, or have caused some misunderstanding, or have forgotten some occasion or appointment that is important to their wives, who respond to these transgressions with shrugs and eye rolls. The audience laughs and applauds at both the transgressions and the reactions. She thinks it would be easier on both her and her husband if she could react with such bemused resignation to his shortcomings, or if their disagreements resulted in laughter and applause. Maybe they should fight in front of a studio audience from now on. She's extraordinarily comfortable right now. Indeed, the husband pillow is more comfortable than her husband, than any husband, would be in this situation. For the purpose of watching sitcom episodes on her laptop, this husband is superior to her husband.

This line of thinking makes her feel guilty, so she calls her husband. She says, "I'm lying here in bed with my husband!" He seems annoyed. She explains the joke, but he doesn't think it's funny. She has parlayed her pointless guilt into actual, justifiable guilt by turning an imaginary hurt into a real one. She ends the call and leans a little more heavily into the husband pillow.

Then the phone rings in her hand. It's her party husband. He asks what she's doing and she says, "I'm lying in bed with my husband," and he says, "Cool, does he have any weed?" Her party husband is disappointed when she explains. Now she is worried that her party husband likes her husband more than he likes her. It may be true. When her husband is in town, the two spend a lot of time together in the garage. They are each other's weed husband.

She tries, as often as she can stand it, to think of herself as a wife, and to act the way a wife is supposed to act. But she is not sure what way this is. Also, she isn't sure whether her husband wants her to act wifely, or if he simply considers her every action to be wifely, since she is his wife. Or perhaps he doesn't think about things like this at all. He gets frustrated when she tries to talk about them. He doesn't see the point. To be fair, she doesn't either.

Sometimes her loneliness is intense and deeply upsetting. This often happens when her husband is away, but sometimes it happens when he is in town. Sometimes it is at its worst when he is in town and isn't inclined to do the things that she regards as husbandly. At times, her desire for her husband to be husbandly results in the appearance of the fight husband. He wants her to explain what on earth it is she wants him to do, and this is a reasonable request, but often she can't explain. She just wants him to know. She wants him to know so that she doesn't have to know. A husband of this nature would be a magic husband. Once, he even said to her, "I'm not made of magic!" and this phrase, though uttered in anger, struck them both as hilarious, and ended the fight they were having. When they are getting along well and she particularly loves him, she thinks of him as, and sometimes calls him, her magic husband.

In the morning the day after the arrival of the husband pillow, her husband calls and apologizes for the phone conversation of the previous day. She apologizes too. He'll be home soon, he says. When she ends the call, she's happy. He will deliver himself home—he'll be her package husband, delivering the package that is himself to her, and perhaps he will become the sex husband, and if he makes her coffee he can be the coffee husband, and if they go to a party he can be the party husband. He might compliment her and tell her jokes, and be those husbands too.

She has never felt that her husband was, at any particular time, all the husbands at once, all the good ones, but it could happen. It is more likely, anyway, than the other thing that might satisfy her, which would be to have all the other husbands in the house along with him, making her coffee, bringing her packages, having sex with her, being nice, and telling jokes. Of course, all those husbands would have to bring their actual wives or husbands, or else they would be lonely; and of course the real husbands or wives might have many wives or husbands, as she has many husbands, and those wives and husbands would need to bring their actual husbands or wives, and so on. An infinitely crowded house, bulging with exponentially increasing numbers of husbands and wives.

Better to be alone here, with the husband pillow and, eventually, sometimes, the husband. Better to be lonely sometimes, to have to be one's own husband. To be a couple, a couple of one.

Something You May Not Have Known about Vera

I was supposed to meet Vera downtown, at our usual place. It was springtime, and I was taking the bus. The child sitting next to me had removed one of the cold cuts from his bag lunch and was rubbing it against his bare knee. The smell of the processed meat, combined with the odors of insect repellent and sweat, inspired in me a mild nausea. The child offered me the cold cut and I shook my head no.

I turned and looked out the window. The bus was enveloped in a heavy fog, so heavy that I could make out nothing beyond the glass other than a bright and featureless gray. The driver roared along at what was certainly a dangerous speed, given the weather, and I felt anxious.

The bus was a school bus. The boy beside me was named Frank. I was aware of wishing to be elsewhere, with other people, though I couldn't think of whom. Frank poked me on the arm and opened his mouth to speak and static came out.

o

The bus stopped and we lined up to get off. A woman at the door asked each of us a series of questions. Did we have our lunches? Our hats? Had we applied insect repellent, sunscreen? Her face was indistinct; indeed, it was blank, as blank as the bus windows.

I answered yes to her questions and stepped into a brilliant downtown summer afternoon. The fog had lifted. Our usual place was across the street; Vera waved from the table in the window where we liked to sit. I waved back, crossed at the light, and walked in.

From the doorway I could see into the kitchen prep area, tucked into the right rear corner of the restaurant. My mother stood there with her cleaver and white apron, as I had seen her so many times behind the meat counter of the supermarket where she worked when she was alive. She nodded to me with unsmiling good cheer, which was how she signaled our special bond during working hours. My father, I felt, ought to have been holding my hand, but I was alone.

The left rear corner of the restaurant was blank. A word appeared in my field of vision, glowing yellow: SEARCHING. And then another word, LOADING. The words seemed to float about six feet in front of me, four feet off the ground. The second word disappeared and the restaurant corner came into view. It didn't look right. The rear wall seemed to have been demolished, and outside, children were sitting at picnic tables set up in the parking lot. Beyond lay sand, then the sea. I could make out the distant crashing waves.

I felt someone touch my hand and I turned. It was Vera. She kissed me. I had something to ask her. I had something to give her, as well, and it was in my pocket.

o

We'd been dating for a while. A couple of years. Our first date had been a lunch date, right here in this restaurant, and we'd eaten here once a week ever since. We lived within a few blocks of each other and rarely had a night passed that we didn't spend together. We had signaled to each other that we might want to move in together soon. So I'd decided to ask her to marry me. I was certain she'd say yes. In fact, I had a particular surprise for her. It wasn't a ring I had in my pocket. I'd applied to have us uploaded together.

I knew she'd been saving to get uploaded. So had I—indeed, I'd already paid most of my fee and had been partially uploaded already. I was pretty sure that if we pooled our money we would have enough for the couples discount, and could finish together. If she agreed to marry me today, I was going to take my phone out and scan my retina and scan her retina and then validate the application. I would take her on a honeymoon trip to Seattle, and the centerpiece of the trip would be to shuttle out to the suburbs and get her uploaded. This way, when the invasion came, if we both died, as pretty much everyone was expected to, we could be together, as data. It might even be possible to download ourselves into new bodies, at some point in the distant future. The Company had hinted at as much, though it wasn't making any promises. I was a believer, though, both in the Company and in Vera's love.

We sat down and gazed into each other's eyes. Vera was a lovely woman—clear skin, soft hair, a kind and gentle smile. We didn't need to speak—this was our weekly ritual. We just enjoyed being here, together.

I knew what I would order, of course—we both always got the same thing—but I glanced at the menu anyway, for form's sake. Or maybe we'd get an appetizer of some kind, for a change of pace. The menu, however, wasn't working. The stained and sauce-spattered cardstock was empty of lunch options, and instead displayed a single word, repeating at an oblique angle across the page: CORRUPTED CORRUPTED CORRUPTED CORRUPTED. And then, as I watched, a corner of the old menu flickered into place—I caught sight of the words *tofu bibimbap*—before the entire thing was replaced by what seemed to be a news article. The headline read THEY ARE AMONG US, and a photo was displayed beneath it, the blurry image of a man in a suit with some kind of prehensile claw extending from his back.

Vera was speaking now, so I had only a moment to peruse the text of the article; I made out the words *invasion is already in progress* and *assuming human shape* before I turned my attention to her words.

". . . so very nice to see you," she was saying.

"What's that, Love?"

"It is so very nice to see you," she said. She smiled evenly.

I reached out and took her hand. "Well, yes, of course."

Vera had beautiful hands, fine boned yet strong. This one felt cold, though. "Are you all right, Vera?"

Her eyes blinked quickly. "Yes!" she said, and for a moment her hand seemed to flex in mine, to clench and harden, and I pulled away.

Something outside the window caught my attention—a passing white panel van. But it wasn't a van. It was just a solid white van-sized block with the words MISSING ITEM, SUBSTITUTION IN PROGRESS scrolling across its surface, and then it turned into an elephant, an old, tired-looking elephant that I remembered seeing at the zoo when I was a child. It lumbered around the corner, not seeming to notice that it was out of place on the city street, and passersby didn't seem to notice it either.

That's when I felt Vera's hand on mine, and I knew without looking that it wasn't a hand at all, but a claw. When I turned to her, her eyes were white discs, each bearing the three pixelated platonic shapes of the familiar broken-image symbol, and behind her my mother was standing on an empty table with her cleaver, cutting my brother down from the ceiling fan he had hanged himself from. *I don't want to be here for the invasion,* his note read. My mother turned to me, startled, and her gaze was full of the misery and remorse that would lead her to do the same, some weeks later. I missed them both.

o

I suddenly remembered, as Vera produced the glowing cylinder with her other claw, where we had been going on that field trip, when I sat next to Frank Cousins on the bus. It was to the beach, a spring outing to the beach, but it had been marred by a massive die-off of some kind of crab—horseshoe crabs, I'd guess. Their shells littered the sand, and they stank in the sun, and I never forgot the way the shells felt under my fingers, the exoskeletons, and I took comfort now in knowing that the invasion had already occurred, that they had taken Vera first, and that the Company had come through in the end. That, in some sense, I lived still.

The Deaths of Animals

When we moved to the edge of town, we adopted two cats. We had previously decided not to keep cats anymore, but now that we lived close to the countryside, on some land, in a house set far back from the road, we imagined that the cats, once they were old enough to be let outside, would enjoy the chance to hunt and roam. So we drove to the pound with the children and chose two cats, and brought them home, and gave them names.

Let us call them Cat A and Cat B.

The two cats were great friends. One (Cat B) was mercurial, sleek and black, difficult to please. The other (Cat A) was striped, stocky, and friendly. They grew together out of kittenhood, and once we had acclimated them to their environment, we let them out. They were habitual, charming animals. They stayed away from the road. They generally left the house together and returned together as well. Months passed.

One evening, Cat B returned at the usual time, in response to our calls to dinner, but Cat A did not. It was dark outside. We called and called. Eventually we went to bed.

When we awoke, Cat A was still missing. It was while waiting with the children for the school bus that we noticed his body lying at the side of the road, forty yards to the west. The children boarded the bus. The bus pulled away and passed Cat A's lifeless form as they gazed out the window. We collected the corpse and buried it in the back yard.

We were convinced the incident was a fluke. We would like to point out that we had had many outdoor cats in the past, in homes situated much closer to the road, and had never lost one to passing traffic. Our previous cat—let us call her Cat X—had used to lie in the grass on the verge sloping down from the busy street near our former tiny house, and she would place her head on her paws and peer at the passing cars. She was not, in most ways, a satisfactory cat, but her caution around cars was admirable. She died of illness.

We assumed, you see, that Cat X, not Cat A, was the correct model for predicting the behavior of cats in the vicinity of busy roads.

For this reason we thought it sensible to acquire Cat C. Cat C was entirely gray, plaintive, and cute. If you stood before him with one foot extended on the floor, he would wiggle his haunches, dash up your leg, vault over your chest, and settle on your shoulders, where he would rest as you walked about the house. But Cat C was not intelligent. He would beg for food, even if food was already on his plate. He seemed to forget what time of day it was and what was expected of him. Cat B prided himself on his intelligence and reliability, and resisted Cat C's overtures of friendship for some time. But eventually the two became inseparable.

We let Cat C outside.

Because, you must understand, it is not possible, or in any event not practical, to have two cats, one allowed out, the other not. It did cross our minds that Cat C's stupidity and resistance to habit might present a risk, once he was allowed out. But Cat B seemed eager to go outdoors with his friend, imagining, we guessed, that the two would spend time together there, as they did inside the house.

But Cat C did not remain with his friend. Instead, he ran about with wild abandon. He proved to have no sense of direction, no instinct for home. We searched for him every night, finding him on the neighbors' back stoops, on the playground of a school, on the lowest branches of a distant tree.

Cat C had no boundaries. One of the two of us, who also had no boundaries, found this quality amusing, and remained blithely confident that Cat C would always return, and deserved the chance to roam. The other of us liked this quality in Cat C no more than she liked it in the first of us, and indeed seemed to regard the wanderings of the first of us and those of Cat C with similar feelings of irritation and dread.

Eventually a neighbor called us with the news that a mangled gray form resembling Cat C was visible in the road outside her house.

At this point it is reasonable to ask what one imagines we might have done, given that Cat B had lived his entire life as an outdoor cat, and had grown accustomed to the pleasures of the outdoors. To shut him in, we believed, would be cruel. And of course Cat B was a survivor; he was wily and cautious, and he ran away in fear anytime we pulled our car into and out of the driveway.

Cats A and C were flukes, we maintained. Cat B exhibited the "correct" behavior, as previously exemplified by Cat X. Thus, Cat B was allowed outside once again.

In the subsequent two years, Cat B grew less mercurial, more openly affectionate, a bit heavier. He hunted daily. He was declared, by the two of us, to be the "best cat ever." He was praised by one of us for lacking the boundary problems that had beset both Cat C and the other of us. The other of us had finally agreed that these were indeed problems in a cat, though was reluctant to admit that they were problems in a human.

However, the same one of us with the aforementioned boundary problems, who maintained privately that they were not actually problems, found himself one week outside the good graces of the other of us, owing precisely to those boundary problems, which he was now forced, at long last, to admit were actually problems in humans as well as cats. And so things were already not so good when we discovered Cat B's body in the street, not less than ten feet from where, years before, we had discovered the body of Cat A.

Our immediate impulse was to blame our neighbor, owing to an incident that had occurred only a few weeks before, in which six of our free-range chickens were killed by a dog while we were at the movies. A trail of feathers led from our yard, where dead chickens were strewn about like tree limbs after a thunderstorm, straight down the driveway, across the street, and into the neighbors' driveway. This neighbor most certainly did have a dog, a dog with boundary problems, who could often be seen pacing along the side of the road, having escaped from her pen; we were quite certain that this was the dog to blame. The one of us with boundary problems had planned, after burying the dead chickens, to confront the neighbor with this evidence, but before he got a chance, the neighbor came over on her own and admitted that she had just watched her boundary-problem-beset dog shake to death one of our chickens on her own property.

Well, the one of us with boundary problems said, your dog with boundary problems actually killed five more of our chickens.

The neighbor reiterated that her dog had certainly killed one chicken, and she was sorry for that, but perhaps it was that chicken who had had the boundary problem, not her dog, because as far as we knew the chicken might have crossed the road of its own volition, exciting the dog and inviting attack.

In response to this implausible scenario, the one of us with boundary problems inquired how, then, the other five chickens might have died, to which the neighbor responded that, in the end, there was really no way to know, was there? And she again hinted that the chickens themselves were to blame, implying that they were not, in fact, free-range chickens but boundary-problem chickens, and then she thanked herself for burying the single dead chicken in her yard instead of carrying it over to our house and handing it to us, and she turned around and went home.

And so, as we were still angry at the neighbor for her boundary problems, and for her dog's boundary problems, and for accusing our chickens of having boundary problems, and as the one of us with boundary problems was presently outside the good graces of the other of us precisely because of those boundary problems, we entered into a state of denial, and temporarily convinced ourselves that

Cat B, who had clearly developed boundary problems, had in fact been lured out of his normal state of being by, and was perhaps even run over by, the boundary-problem-beset, dog-owning neighbor.

However, since Cat B's body had been lying to the west of the neighbor's driveway, and construction, at this time, blocked the road to the west of Cat B's body, it seemed highly unlikely that our neighbor would have had any reason to drive to the place where Cat B was killed. So we let go of our anger and buried Cat B and told the children the bad news, and vowed never to have cats again.

And in much the same way, the one of us with boundary problems vowed never to have boundary problems again, and the other of us grudgingly accepted this promise, vaguely recalling that she had heard it before, but unsure of what else she was supposed to do. And now when the children leave the house every day, we are tempted to drag them back inside and lock the door, to tell them that they are indoor children now, to establish clear and immovable boundaries, but we resist, understanding that no boundary is either clear or immovable, which of course is the entire reason any man or creature ever has problems with them. We just tell the children to be careful, and stay away from traffic, and we are sorry, so sorry, that we exposed them with such depressing regularity to the deaths of animals.

FIVE

It's Over

She said, "We're through," and I said, "I don't know how to put this, but I think we should start seeing—" and she interrupted, saying, "We have to talk," and I smashed the wineglass against the wall and said, "I can't stand another day with you!" She looked me in the eye and said, "I'm not in love with you anymore," and I said, "We've changed, feelings change," and she said, "After talking to my therapist, I've made a decision," and I said, "I've spoken to a lawyer and I think you should too." "You're fucking her, aren't you," she replied, and I said, "How long have you been seeing him?" She took the ring off and said, "I think you should have this back," and I took the ring off and said, "I've been living a lie," and we handed each other the rings, then we went to bed and we cried out other people's names during sex and afterward she said, "I don't think I can do this anymore," and I turned away from her and said, "I don't know how to say this, but." She went to sleep on the couch and I went to sleep on the other couch and in the morning, over coffee, we gently looked each other in the eye and said, "It's over," and prepared ourselves for another day.

By the Light of Small Explosions

Something happens when the sign comes into view on the other side of the hill. The sign says WEST LAKE RECREATION AREA, but he can't *read* it. His family is with him in the car: Lori and the children. They're headed for the West Lake Recreation Area and he knows it's along here somewhere, they're close, and it seems likely the sign they're approaching is the one they have been looking for. He understands the individual words; that the sign, in theory, refers, or should refer, to a large inland body of water, and to the discharge of free time, and to a certain demarcation of land; and that something is supposed to lie to the west of something else. But his mind cannot assimilate the disparate words into a full unit of meaning. Something in the mental process that used to cleave ideas together has reversed its polarity, and the harder he struggles to push these concepts into cognitive proximity, the more they repel one another. His vision blurs (and, far to one side, brightens, by the light of small explosions, little bursts of eerie blue-white), and he says, with difficulty, "Does it . . . ?" and Lori says "Dan!" and the car declines to respect the curve of the road and they dip down, then up, and the children scream as the blue explosions fill his field of vision, bringing with them the smell of the wooden horse's mane, the one from the carousel at Stevens Park that, as a child, crying, he wouldn't get off of until his stepfather arrived to peel him away, saying, "Come on, now, Danny, come now. Your mother's waiting, Danny, don't make it hard for everyone. Don't make it hard.."

Death (Movie)

I went to the movies with my teenage child and my adult child. An adventure movie, about gigantic animals living on a remote island. But not a movie for children. The actors said fuck and some of them were torn limb from limb before our eyes.

Nevertheless, a small child was sitting behind us. It had come with its parents, to whom it was directing a fairly constant stream of commentary. "It's a spider!" the child said. "The helicopter crashed!" "The monkey is really mad!"

Eventually I turned around and told it to stop talking. For the remainder of the movie, I felt bad about having done so. Had I embarrassed the child, its parents? And my own children—did I seem crazy to them now? Perhaps they were thinking, No wonder he doesn't live with our mother anymore.

I took comfort, though, in having quelled at last not only the child, but my fervent hope that, like the creatures and characters in the film, it might suddenly just die.

Death (After)

I believe in the afterlife in the same way I believe in the afterparty: it may exist, but I'm not invited, and so will never find out.

Death (Something)

My friend, also a writer, died. He was dead for only a short while—less than a minute. Heart stopped, brain activity ceased; the doctors stepped away from the table. Then the machines started screaming and my friend shuddered back to life.

His writing changed after that. It got stupider, frankly. He sold a lot of books and got laid. Everybody wanted to talk about what was on the other side. Was there a light? Did he meet God? He really hammed it up at readings, this story (it was a snakebite, by the way, out in some national park), and I hated him for it, but I coveted his friendship more than ever, because he had been touched by, I don't know, something. Something different from loneliness, or shaving cream, or a dog's tongue flecked with kibble.

But he said to me, "Honestly, it was nothing. Literally. I woke up and I felt like shit and I couldn't even remember the snakebite."

He said, "Maybe I'm dead. Maybe this is death."

"Wouldn't that be something," he said. "If you don't even know you're dead unless somebody tells you it happened."

Apparently Not

Could it be that he really did remember to put the chains on the truck tires, that she came back from the valley with the baby formula as expected, in spite of the freak snowstorm, and nursed the child, nursed him that night and each night for the next three months at the appointed hour, the hour when once again tonight he feels her hand on his shoulder and rouses from sleep to find her standing over him, blankly beseeching, wondering where the child has gone, not realizing that the child is living with her parents now, that he couldn't raise the child on his own, that he has since that night been incapable even of cooking his own meals in this empty cottage in the woods at the top of the hill that their trucked slipped and swerved on, and off of which it tumbled in the snow all the way to the creek below; could it be that he has dreamed these terrible months of loneliness and guilt, that this is not her ghost, that this hand is corporeal, that the cold bed is an illusion and she has touched him only to acknowledge him as she rises to gather the child from the crib?

No, apparently not.

Mud

What you were thinking as the railing collapsed and you and the child tumbled together into the lake: what would she remember of these days of slammed doors and late-night shouts, of furtive phone calls, drunkenness, sudden fits of sobbing, mysterious absences—would she look back in anger, or with pity? Would she talk shit about you to her lovers and friends, or wish, at some desperate juncture, never to have been born?

But years later, in a wine bar of her stepmother's choosing, in the city where she and her wife lived, she would tell you nothing of her memories, would carefully avoid any statement that might be perceived as incriminating her mother (evidence of a maturity that might have told you more about her than her childhood memories would have, had you been paying attention), only remarking, in a world-weary tone that made you wish you hadn't come or at least that you hadn't brought your wife along with you, that until that day at the lake, she had imagined that every body of water harbored an unimaginable beauty and complexity, idealized peaceful, subaquatic civilizations living in majestic natural opulence, mermen and mermaids riding eight-foot seahorses to grand aquatic ballrooms; but on that day she learned that water was hostile and dangerous and that there was nothing down there at all, she said, with a lingering glance at your wife, who was typing something furiously on her phone, nothing down there but cold and death and mud.

Marriage (Divorce (Pie))

He says, So that's it?

That's it, she says.

It's over, you're saying.

That's what I'm saying, she says.

He stares at her, and she stares back. It's a staring contest. She wins. He looks down at his hands, which are tightly clenched on the kitchen table.

Well, now what, he says.

She says, One of us has to move out.

Well, it isn't going to be me, he says.

It's going to have to be, she says, because it isn't going to be me, and that leaves you.

I found this place, he says.

I make more money than you, she says.

He says, But I paid more of the down payment.

With money you owed me, she says. Because I helped you buy the scooter.

We co-owned the scooter!

You're the one who used it, she says.

He says, You're the one who wrecked it!

That's your fault, she says. You didn't tell me it needed new tires.

It didn't!

Anyway, she says, getting up, this place is closer to my office than it is to yours. You'll want a place near your office.

Says who! I like walking from here!

No, you don't, she says. You hate it. You always complain about the panhandlers and the hipsters and the loud buses.

Those are general complaints about city life, he explains.

Well, she says. Maybe you should move away from the city, then. You could rent a cabin somewhere. Write that novel you always wanted to write.

Novel?

Yeah, she says. The Great American Novel.

I don't want to write any novel, he says.

Sure you do, she says, walking out of the room. Everybody wants to write the Great American Fucking Novel.

o

He follows her into the bedroom, where she is lying down, reading a magazine. He says, So who's going to call June and Theo?

What do you mean?

To tell them we're not coming, he says.

Who said anything about that?

He stares at her. She stares back. It's a staring contest. She wins. He looks at her feet, which are motionless and bare, and says, We're divorcing. We're not going to spend the weekend visiting June and Theo.

Of course we are, she says.

Well, you can, he says. I'm staying here.

No, you're not, she says. Theo is your friend. We've been avoiding this visit for months. Now we have to go.

We don't have to do anything!

You're going to need friends after we divorce, she says. Theo's been divorced. You can talk about that. Out on the back patio, drinking whiskey. You can tell him what a horrible bitch I am.

He already knows that, he says.

She says, Touché.

If anything, he says, you should stay home. You can't stand June.

That's not true, she says, weakly.

After they left here last time, you said she was the shallowest cunt in Pennsylvania.

She chuckles. Yes, she says, I did.

So why do you want to go?

I'm going to need friends too, she says, and turns the page of her magazine.

June? You want June to be your friend?

Of course, she says. I don't want friends who are smarter than I am. I want friends I can manipulate.

Well, he says, at least you're being honest.

She says, My honesty is one of my best qualities.

That's true.

And one of yours is your willingness to admit defeat.

That's true.

You'd better pack, she says. And then you can sleep on the couch.

Why do you get the bed? he asks her.

She cracks her toes. I'm already on it, she says. Do you want to try to take it from me?

He tries to think of a witty retort. After a few moments, he admits defeat and goes to the closet to pack.

o

She drives. In the car, she swears at other motorists inside the city limits, and then she swears at them on the expressway, and then she swears at them on the divided highway that leads to June and Theo's house. Eventually they are on a road too remote to be burdened with traffic, and she swears at the woods.

Look at that fucking shit, she says. It's full of serpents and trolls. And deer, probably.

What's wrong with deer? he says, glumly.

Are you going to tell me you like deer now? she shouts. Obviously your head's so full of sentimental Bambi-ass bullshit that you can't see the truth. Which is that deer are the fucking roaches of the forest.

They're disease-ridden tick magnets and their meat tastes like flop sweat. Imagine living out here, surrounded by the things. Human-sized rats with fucking coat racks on their heads.

You're in a good mood, he says.

Her face makes something like a smile. I am, she says.

Why? he asks her. Everything is terrible.

I guess I'm contemplating life alone in the house, without you.

He says, Oh.

I'm going to strew magazines everywhere, lying open to the articles I'll never finish reading. I'm going to spill coffee on things and just leave it there. I shall fart openly, in whatever room I want, and I'll get to do whatever I like, whenever I like, which is basically nothing, all the time.

Sounds great.

It is, she says. It is great. It is my future. As soon as we get through this bullshit weekend with our garbage friends.

You're the one who insisted on going, he says. I was content to stay home.

You shouldn't call it home anymore, she says. You're moving out.

I haven't agreed to that.

Sure you have.

No, I haven't.

She shrugs. You have in your mind, she says. It's as good as done.

He considers replying, then decides against it. Instead, he presses his forehead to the window and stares out at the deer-infested woods.

o

The sight of June and Theo's house fills him with dread. It is large and tidy and situated on a cul-de-sac in a quasi-suburban neighborhood near the college where Theo teaches economics. He went to school with Theo—they played Ultimate Frisbee together, an athletic contest for people who like to smoke weed and drink themselves stupid. Neither he nor Theo do these things much anymore, but Theo likes to pretend that drunken, stoned antics are forever just around the corner. This is annoying, but Theo is the only friend he has who makes any kind of effort with him, and he feels duty-bound to respond in kind.

June, a fussy, pretty woman who wears a lot of jewelry, meets them at the door and says, Look at you! Just look at you two!

He glances at his wife, afraid of what she will say. What she says is, Look at you!

No, I mean, just look at you! June says.

No, look at you!

June appears uncomfortable. She turns to lead them into the house, and he elbows her.

Why did you do that? she says, loudly enough for June to hear. Why did you hit me with your elbow?

Sorry, he says.

Theo greets them in the kitchen. He is wearing a big, floppy hat. My dermatologist told me it was time! he says. I'm getting to be that age!

She says, To wear hats indoors?

Haha! Theo says. We can always count on you for a laugh! Can't we, June?

We sure can, June says without enthusiasm.

Theo takes a couple of beers out of the fridge and beckons him out to the patio. He follows, glancing at his wife over his shoulder. She is eyeing June hungrily. A few moments later he and Theo are sitting on a pair of cushioned chairs facing the trees. He thinks, I'm not going to tell Theo we're getting divorced. It's too painful to discuss.

Haha, remember Zoober? Theo says. Remember Kwan? Remember that one time?

Haha, yeah, he replies.

Theo says, Man, where did Lopez get that sweet bud, am I right? I couldn't tell my ass from my ankle.

We're getting divorced, he says.

What! Theo exclaims. You two?

He nods.

I thought you two would be together forever!

Really? he says. We fight constantly and are unpleasant to be around. When we announced our engagement, everyone agreed that our union would be an expensive mistake.

Sure, but still, says Theo.

How do you and June do it? he asks. You seem so happy.

Oh, I dunno, Theo says, gesturing with his bottle of beer. Stamina. Inertia. We've had a rough patch here and there.

What kind of rough patch?

Oh, Theo says, you know. June's a hypochondriac and shoplifts, and I don't like sex. But we're pretty solid, I think.

Right.

So, Theo goes on, clearing his throat, what's next for you two? Is she moving out?

He takes a sip of his beer, which turns into a long draught, which turns into the bottle being empty. No, he says glumly. I am.

○

In the kitchen, she is listening to June talk. June is making a pie, but this isn't preventing her from also talking. June is multitasking, with the two tasks being talking and making a pie. June says, I've been to four doctors and none of them can figure out what's going on with my neck.

I was going to say, she replies. What's up with her neck? I asked myself.

June says, Really? You noticed?

It's in your carriage, she says. I took one look at you and I thought, That neck is super wrong.

June is energetically crumbling cold butter into a bowl of flour. June says, It's just like what happened with my bowels last year. I can't tell you how many colonoscopies I had. Have you ever had one?

Oh, haven't we all, she says.

So then you know, June says. Sorry I have to do this now, June adds. It's for my bereavement group tomorrow.

So it isn't for us, then? You're making a pie, but not for us?

Yeah, no, like I said, June says, turning to a bowl of fruit and slicing it into pieces. There's ice cream in the freezer for you. For after dinner. Which I think Theo is grilling.

We're getting divorced, she says.

I'm mostly over Kibble's passing, June says, cutting fruit, but the group is still very helpful. And I think I'm helping others by being there. I thought about canceling tomorrow, being as you're here, but Theo said to me, June, no, they need you, your experiences are valuable to the group. So I'm making this pie. I'm sorry, what did you say?

We're getting—

June silences her with a hand. She has suddenly frozen in place, her head at a strange angle. June says, Oh God. See? Oh, holy mother of Jesus. My neck.

The knife clatters into the fruit bowl. June's hands are crabbed and trembling. She speaks through gritted teeth.

Help me out here. Hey. Would you?

She gets up from her seat and moves over to the kitchen island, then places her hands on June's shoulders. She massages them gently, then firmly. She moves her fingers up to June's neck and squeezes and probes. June groans and lets out a small, plaintive squeal.

Thank you. Oh, thank you, June says.

No problem, she replies.

o

After a dinner of some kind of casserole and some kind of salad, and a dessert of frost-furred vanilla ice cream from the freezer, the four of them take a walk along the footpaths through the woods. June and Theo forge ahead, carrying polished walking sticks they made themselves from fallen branches. June is limping and saying something about her knee, and Theo nods as if he's listening.

She and he lag behind. He says something to her in a low grumble that she can't quite hear.

What? she says. Speak up.

I said, he says, I want the sofa. It's the best sofa I've ever had, and it's mine, and I'm going to take it.

In that case, she says, I get the camera.

It's not *the* camera, he says, it's *my* camera. You don't even use it.

I think I will, from now on, she says.

No, you won't! he says. You'll never take pictures of things, because you don't like them. Things. You hate them!

She says, I think I'll learn to appreciate things by photographing them, with my camera.

Fine, he says. You can keep the sofa.

Oh, good. And the camera? she says.

No, not the camera! he says.

I think I'll keep the sofa and the camera, she says, as though to herself. That's a nice combination.

He stares at her, and, after a moment, she stares back. It's a staring contest. She wins. They walk together in silence for a while and then he says, Theo tells me that he doesn't like sex and that June shoplifts.

Don't judge, she replies.

You don't get to tell me that! he says. You are literally the most judgmental person I have ever known! Anyway, I'm not judging, I'm just saying.

She says, By the way, June made you a pie.

Really? he says. That pie is for me?

She told me it was, she says.

He says, What kind of pie is it?

Fruit.

I like fruit, he says.

I think she wants to sleep with you, she says. On account of Theo not liking sex. The pie is a metaphor.

It's also a pie, though, he says.

It's both.

They walk in silence for a while until her face makes something like a smile and she points and says, Look! A deer!

○

He wakes up in the middle of the night and can't get back to sleep. It's cooler out in the country, among the trees, so Theo and June keep the air-conditioning off and the windows open. The open windows disturb him, and the night sounds of the forest disturb him, and his estranged wife's presence in the bed disturbs him, though her absence from it would probably disturb him more.

Oh, well, he thinks. He'll have to get used to it.

After a while he gets out of bed and tiptoes down the dark stairs to the kitchen. He opens the refrigerator and takes out a carton of milk. He pours himself a glass and microwaves it until it's warm. Then he takes a seat at the table and sips his warm milk.

It's then that he notices the fruit pie, which has been left on the table to cool in the shadows. It's beautifully made, with a crusty brown lattice supporting lots of little pastry leaves. From underneath them the fruity filling has bubbled up and settled, leaving syrupy traces that are probably sweet and chewy.

He thinks of what his estranged wife has told him, and goes to the cabinet for a plate. He finds a fork and a cake server and uses these items to serve himself a large piece of the fruit pie.

It's delicious. He eats the entire piece, washing it down with warm milk, and when he's finished he gets up and helps himself to more milk and more pie.

Halfway through the second piece, though, he is interrupted by June, who has moved stealthily into the moonlit room. She has a strange bearing; her arms are extended and bent, as though supporting a large tureen filled to the brim with hot soup. She is mumbling to herself and, in her sheer nightgown, looks very attractive.

He realizes that, though her eyes are open, June is asleep. She's sleepwalking. She drifts over to the kitchen island and speaks incoherently while making motions with her hands. She would seem to be pantomiming the acts of cooking and complaining.

Impulsively, he stands up and goes to her. Her takes her by the shoulders and speaks her name. Then he takes her into his arms and begins to kiss her on the mouth. For a few seconds her lips move as if in response to his kisses, but he soon realizes that she has merely continued to talk. He experimentally fondles her breast, and she wakes up and takes an awkward step back.

What are you doing! Where am I! What's happening!

He doesn't know what to say, so he just stands there.

Did you touch me! Did you kiss me! Why are you in my kitchen!

I couldn't sleep, he says. I came down and ate some pie.

What pie!

The fruit pie, he says. It's delicious.

Still blinking away sleep, she glances frantically around the room. Her gaze lands on the half-eaten pie and half glass of milk and she emits a piercing shriek.

My pie! You ate my pie!

It's very good, he reiterates.

It's for my group! My bereavement group! You ate my pie! You kissed me!

Well, he says.

You grabbed my tit! You ate my pie!

What's going on? demands Theo, who has just entered the room wearing a union suit and an actual peaked nightcap, like a character in a Christmas movie. He flicks a switch and the room is bathed in light. June? he says. Is everything all right?

June points and says, He ate my pie, violated my personal boundaries, and woke me up while I was sleepwalking!

Did you wake my wife up from sleepwalking? Theo says angrily.

I suppose so, he admits.

Don't you know how dangerous that is? That's my wife! Theo shouts. This is my house!

These statements are superfluous both in the volume with which they are spoken and the information they convey. He says, I know. I'm sorry.

People have been known to suffer cardiac arrest when awakened from sleepwalking! Theo loudly informs them.

Also, June adds, I've been personally violated! And my pie!

I think you need to leave, Theo says, then adds, And to think we were once Ultimate buddies. We went through that thing together that one time! I can't believe it.

I'm sorry, he says again. Then he hears the voice of his estranged wife.

What the fuck is going on here? she demands, coming down the stairs.

Theo and June explain the situation, accurately, if overemphatically.

She nods, listening, and then turns to him. She says, How can you be friends with these ridiculous fuckwads?

Theo says, Hey—

I've never met a more irritating, self-deluding couple of back-woods dumbasses in my entire life, she says. She turns to him. Was this garbage the best your stupid college had to offer? You'd've been better off making friends with the fucking frisbee.

She addresses herself to Theo. You, she says. You're a pathetic ex-cuse for a man. You sound like a cockatoo and you look like a fuck-ing Hummel figurine. Talking with you is like being smothered in your sleep with a pillow. You should cut your dick off and feed it to a dog.

And you, she says, turning to June, are a miserable shit with the IQ of a box turtle and a butt like a paper sack of doughnut holes. You dress like you're in a Laura Ingalls Wilder fetish porno. The most important thing in your life is a dead cat, and your bathroom is dirty.

This man, she shouts now, pointing, is my husband. He is a thou-sand times the human being either of you will ever be, and you should be dry-humping the ground he walks on. You don't deserve to have your boob grabbed by him, your fucking nature trail walked on by him, or your pie eaten by him. If I ever catch either one of you so much as giving him the stink eye, you will find my Doc Martens ankle-deep in your hemorrhoid-encrusted assholes so fast you'll won-der if you just time-traveled back to freshman year at fisting school.

Husband! she commands, pointing to the stairs. Get our bags. We are leaving this shitbox in five minutes.

In the stunned silence that follows, she sits down at the kitchen table, picks up the fork, and begins to eat what is left of the fruit pie.

○

In the car, she says, It was nice catching up with them.

Thank you, he says. For defending me.

She says, You're welcome. I guess you can keep the sofa.

And the camera?

And the camera.

Well, he says. Thanks for that too.

Or, she says.

Or?

We could just stay married.

He doesn't say anything for a moment. The dark woods rush by outside.

Is that what you want? he asks her.

What I want, she says, is for the world to not be such a fucking kingdom of shit, and for all the assholes to dry up and blow away. I want all pain to be erased from my memory, and I want to spend the next fifty years in a state of effortless euphoria until I die peacefully in my sleep and ascend to a heaven of puffy clouds, cute interspecies animal friendships, and incessant orgasms at the nimble hands of the men's Olympic diving team.

Okay, he says.

Also, that pie, she says. I want to eat more of that dumb bitch's pie.

I think, he says, that your other wishes might be more easily fulfilled.

Her face makes something like a smile. His does too. He stares at her, and she stares back. It's a staring contest. Then a deer leaps onto the road and is briefly illuminated by their headlights before tumbling over the hood and crashing into the windshield.

The airbags deploy, catching their bodies as they lurch forward together.

Choirboy

The day after the day I turned seventeen, three weeks after the re-
cital in which I received the award for distinguished effort in a solo
violin performance, five months after my older brother was arrested
for dealing cocaine and thrown out of college and came home and
ever since had been living in his old attic room, which he had transformed into his personal domain during the last semester of high
school, when he had the argument with our father that our mother
believed had contributed, however indirectly, to the stroke that
killed Dad some weeks later, I stood on the stair landing, gazing out
through the tiny hexagonal window overlooking the back yard and
saw my mother gardening there, and her bent form among the vege-
tables moved me, yes, but in an unexpected way—somehow the
sight of her vertebrae humped underneath her purple blouse and
the thick white bra strap visible through the fabric, even from here,
filled me with anger, for the way she had pushed me, the way she
had forced me to practice the same pieces over and over again on
those cold afternoons when I was sitting alone beside the radiator,
perspiring through my thick sweatshirt, "You have to do this," she
would tell me, "because you are capable of doing this, your brother
is useless, he has squandered whatever talents he once had, whatever they might have been, he has squandered his youth, sitting
in his room, smoking and listening on headphones to the garbage

music your father lets him buy with the money from that asinine job your father let him take at the mall," which is to say at the pizza place, which is also where he met the stoners who sold him pot, and within months he had climbed over them to their dealer, whom my brother convinced to branch out into cocaine; and though my mother was frail already at forty-eight, worn down by my father's relentless belittlement, I wanted to march down the stairs and tell her she had ruined me, that I hated her, to smash my violin against the cracked and disintegrating concrete cherub that stood in the center of her flower garden, which my father had bought her in a happier time, or perhaps in a time in which unhappiness was still latent, not yet fully expressed—but instead I reached out to the squat and ugly little end table that stood in the corner of the landing and took into my hand the nearest of her china figurines, all of them together a mystery, for they were cheap and tacky and beneath her deluded sense of herself as the wife of a man of wealth and power, which my father was not; rather, he was a second-rate businessman in a third-rate city, and in any event dead now for three years; and when my brother came loping down the stairs from his room, reeking of weed and holding between his chin and extended left hand an imaginary violin, which he limp-wristedly sawed at with the imaginary bow in his right, while emitting a mocking squeak intended to represent my playing at its worst, I turned to him and punched him with all the strength I could muster, shattering both his nose and the choirboy figurine in my hand—and my brother fell back against the stairs, gagging on blood, and I felt the shards of choirboy slice through my palm and the muscles of my fingers, which even at that moment I understood would take six months to heal, if they ever healed at all, ending my nascent career as a classical performer, and I wish I could say that it was with satisfaction that I regarded my brother lying on the carpeted stairs with his hand over his other hand over his face, and that it was with relief that I regarded my ruined hand as the fingers jerked open, raining blood and choirboy pieces onto the oriental runner, but in fact I felt neither; I felt only the foolishness that accompanies any discharge of rage, and the very beginnings of shame, while my mother, as though sensing this disturbance through the hexagonal glass and sixty feet of late-spring air, turned her kerchiefed head to squint up at the house, where everything she had hoped would make her happy was continuing to fall apart.

Candle

Halfway through the second movement, she shudders. She forgot something at home, something important. What is it? Did she shut the back window, lock the front door?

Yes. She did. And the bedroom light was switched off, and the porch light switched on: she remembers making it so. She pulled out of the garage and shut the garage door with the plastic remote. She knows it because she paused in the street until the door was shut, to make sure that a prowler wasn't slipping inside from a hiding place in the shrubs.

What is it, then? She bends over in her seat, straining to remember. The orchestra, which moments before enthralled her utterly, now registers as distracting noise. The stranger beside her, an old man attending the concert with his wife, taps her shoulder, offers an inquiring look. Is she all right? Yes, yes. Leave me alone, let me think.

The concert hall is dimly lit by chandeliers. No, it isn't. But it is the kind of place that might be. Why did she picture them there, dangling overhead, when she knows they aren't there?

That's it! A candle. She left a candle burning in the bedroom, on her makeup table. She meant to blow it out, but, distracted by her clothes and the lateness of the hour, she didn't. It was burning when she left the room! She begins to panic. What if the cat were to knock it over? What if it tumbles onto the rocking chair, where a dress and a quilt are draped, and lights them on fire?

But no, that's not possible. Why not? The candle isn't on the table anymore. It isn't, because she knocked it over with her elbow. The candle fell onto the chair, still burning, and the dress, the vintage rayon dress, caught fire. The dress ignited the cotton quilt, and the quilt ignited the curtains, the wallpaper.

That's what she has been trying to remember. It's almost a relief to know. The house is burning. It was on fire when she left. She watched it from the street, wondering what to do. In the end, she drove away. She went to the concert.

She begins to laugh. The house is burning! By now, perhaps, it's burned up. The old man is still looking at her, his wife too. She shakes her head. No, no. It's fine. She remembers now. It's all gone. There's nothing to be done. She sits back and listens to the music.

Circuit City

Because we didn't like John, our manager, and because we suspected that he planned to rob Circuit City on its final day of operations, we decided (John, John, and I) to rob Circuit City on its final day of operations.

John had been tasked with selling off all stock, which meant deep discounts for our customers on computers, televisions, stereo equipment, video games, DVDs, and home appliances. John elected to close Circuit City for one week leading up to its final day of operations, which was Sunday, March 8, 2009, to generate excitement and to promote the store clearance as a "sales event." The "sales event" would be cash-only, which is an unorthodox procedure at Circuit City and which tipped John, John, and myself off to the possibility that John was planning to rob Circuit City. In movies and on television, which John, John, and I often were able to watch during our shifts at Circuit City, owing to its recent decline in revenue, this is known as a "heist."

"Cash," John observed, smoking, during our smoke break out on the loading dock, "is harder to account for than other forms of payment."

"John is going to steal some or all of the cash," John replied, smoking.

Smoking, I said, "If John intends to steal some or all of the cash, then we should steal some or all of the cash instead." In movies and on television, this is known as a "double cross."

We were wearing the red shirts required of all employees. John wore the required red shirt as well, but upon his required shirt was embroidered the word MANAGER. Because we didn't like John, we called him Manager.

"Manager, this customer is looking for a game controller."

"Manager, this customer would like to return these cables."

"Manager, your required red shirt is looking fly today."

"Stop calling me that."

"Stop calling me that."

"Stop calling me that."

The "sales event" proved successful. Customers lined up around the building to buy computers, televisions, stereo equipment, video games, DVDs, and home appliances, all the way back to the loading dock where no one was smoking due to the "sales event." Circuit City made $42,738 in the hours until noon, at which time John reduced prices by half; then Circuit City made another $29,722 in the hours until 5 p.m., at which time John reduced prices to 90 percent off; then Circuit City made another $22,835 in the hours before closing, for a grand total of $95,295, which we helped John pack into large canvas sacks. In movies and on television, this is known as "loot."

John, John, and I made to leave Circuit City in John's car, after farewells and thank-yous to John, who for the first time ever we didn't call Manager. John appeared moved but eager for us to leave, presumably because John was also eager to transfer the large canvas sacks of dollars into his car. We came back five minutes later to find John at the loading dock, loading the large canvas sacks of dollars into his car.

"Manager, what are you doing?"

"Manager, are those the dollars?"

"Manager, this is an unorthodox procedure."

"Hey well now," John said, and then John pulled a pistol from the crack of his ass and shot John in the head. John collapsed to the ground beside his blood-spattered car, his red shirt, bearing the embroidered word MANAGER, soaked red with blood, which was ironic. The shooting was an unorthodox procedure. In movies and on television, this is known as a "twist." After a moment of reflection, John and I began to transfer the large canvas sacks of dollars from John's car to John's car. John asked John if he intended to help, and John replied, gesturing toward John's lifeless body, "I just did. Also," he said, smoking, which was an orthodox procedure, especially considering that John, John, and I were at the loading dock and were now on what could be termed a permanent smoke break, "it's my car. John," he said, meaning me, "you drive," and he gestured toward the driver's-side door. I got into the car, behind the steering wheel. Driving John's car was an unorthodox procedure. Outside the car, John shot John in much the way he had shot John. Now I understood that John was bad. In the movies and on television, this is known as "anagnorisis."

John climbed into the passenger seat and pointed his pistol at me and said drive. I drove. John said left. John said left. John said right. John said keep going. John said shut up. John said keep going. John said exit. John said right. John said, his voice distorted by the rutted dirt road, keep going.

Now John's portable telephone rang. In movies and on television this is known as "deus ex machina." John looked down. I reached behind my back and pulled out the pistol I'd hidden in the crack of my ass and I pointed it at John. In movies and on television, this is known as "peripeteia." I told John to drop his pistol and instead John pointed his pistol at me, so I shot John, and he shot me. We shot each other. In movies and on television, this is known as "poetic justice." We died.

We kept driving. This was an unorthodox procedure. Our red shirts were red. The dirt road smoothed out and began to glow. Angels appeared on either side of the car to escort us into heaven. In movies and on television, I am known as an "unreliable narrator."

Circuit City was later purchased by Systemax and consolidated, along with CompUSA, into the TigerDirect online brand. This is an orthodox procedure. John and I are still driving. The angels wear red. John and I are beginning to think that they are not angels and that this is not heaven.

The Cottage on the Hill (IV)

And then comes his final visit to the cottage. He is an old man. He would like to see the place one last time. He has spent his declining years doing what he pleases, attended to by people he has hired. His medical care is the best money can buy, and he has been diagnosed with the disease that will kill him. Business has satisfied him, delighted him, even. Everyone he knows, he knows from the world of his work. There have been times when he wished he understood what happened to his family—times when, in dreams, perhaps, or in moments of quiet and calm—he has endured some feeling, some dark sensation, informing him that he was to blame. But these feelings have been few. Richard has put his family behind him, as they have probably done to him.

Still, his desire to see the cottage once more is an acknowledgement that they did mean something to him, and that there is a category of endeavor in which he has been a failure. He does not expect any kind of epiphany; he wants only to see. He wants to see what has changed. So he tells his chief assistant to drive him there, to the old substation, and to let him climb the hill to the cottage.

The substation is entirely gone now—the building, the trailer, the foundation, even the rusted pipes are gone. Instead the hillside is covered with identical white houses, some kind of suburban development, though there is no city near this place, nowhere for the houses' inhabitants to work. The streets are neat and even and climb the hill in gentle switchbacks; they have names like Woodland and Tiger Lily and Knotty Pine.

Richard has brought his cane. His doctor told him not to depend on it for walking, but it doesn't matter now—he won't be walking for much longer. He begins to climb, and as he passes the neat white houses with their paved driveways and fenced yards, he realizes that they have not yet been occupied, that this development is new, built on spec, a work in progress. And the higher he climbs, the smaller these houses become, as if they are a natural phenomenon, responding to the thinness of the air. When he is halfway to the top, the houses are the size of sheds, and then doghouses, and when he is nearly there, they have become dollhouses, miniature houses at the end of miniature sidewalks lining this beautifully paved, full-size street.

He is excited and terrified. His heart thumps and his lungs burn with the crisp air, and he knows that he will never feel this alive again.

The cottage is there, right where it's supposed to be. And it looks as it did the first time, with two stories, and windows, and an oak tree. Except that the walls are gone—or rather they have decayed. It appears that they were made of fabric all along, some kind of canvas, or perhaps it was paper, a paper house, in the Japanese style. Scraps are hanging from the bare beams and flapping in a breeze. Richard walks in through the empty front door frame and stands there, looking up through the roofless roof into the empty sky. The tattered walls flutter all around him.

He tries to remember, but he can't. It isn't as though he's reaching for these elusive memories; it's as though nothing ever happened here to remember. Everything is colorless and odorless, scraped clean by the wind and the rain. He is filled with a deep sense of satisfaction, a deep calm.

And the most extraordinary thing, now, is not the cottage itself but the land beyond it. Because the land has been replaced—the hillside filled in, and built up, and planted with grass and wildflowers.

Indeed, the cottage is no longer at the top of the hill. The hill continues upward, more gently now, and it is lushly meadowed. A path runs away from the cottage up through the meadow, as far as the eye can see. There is a fence up ahead, and a stile to climb over, but the path continues beyond it, into the meadow, without end.

Richard lingers in the cottage for a few minutes more. He has lost his cane, but he feels good enough to walk without it. He turns and looks down at the houses he has passed, the empty houses, foreshortened now with distance so that all of them appear about the same size, the dollhouses and doghouses and sheds and full-size houses, as though they are cardboard cutouts lined up at the back of a makeshift stage where his children are putting on a play. And down below that, tiny now, much like a toy, his big black car, and the assistant waiting for him behind the wheel, his newspaper spread out on the dash.

Richard turns his back on all that, and faces the meadow, and steps out of the cottage through the back wall, the tattered wall that caresses him and gently ushers him into the grass beyond. He begins to climb toward the stile and is treated with the most satisfying feeling, as though the path were made just for him, mowed and graveled for him by a crew of workers, all of them careful not to walk its length as they worked, so as to save that singular experience for him, so that he could be the first. There is new strength in his step, strength to carry him all the way. The air is fresh and scented by the grass, and the fence and the stile are close up ahead, and beyond that is more, something that is his alone, and very soon now he will be there.

Subject Verb

He noticed. He stared. She noticed. She smiled. He approached. She rebuffed. He offered. She accepted. He said, she said, he said, she said. They drank. They said. They drank. He touched. She laughed. They danced. He pressed. She kissed. They went. They did. He left. She slept.

He called. He called. He called. He begged. She refused. He called. He wrote. He visited. He called, called, called, called. She reported. He arrived, shouted, vowed, departed. He plotted. He waited. He visited. She gasped. He demanded. She refused. He grabbed. She screamed. He struck. She ran, locked, called, waited. He panicked. He fled, hid, failed.

She accused. He denied. She described. He denied. She won, he lost.

They aged. She wed, reproduced, parented, saddened, divorced. He bided, waited, hardened. Fought. Smoked. Plotted, planned. Escaped. Vanished.

They lived. She thrived; he faded. He wandered; she traveled.

They encountered.

He sat, she sat. He noticed. She noticed. He gaped. She jumped. She warned; he assured. She reminded; he admitted. She threatened; he promised. She considered. She sat. She asked. He told. He asked. She told. He smoked. She smoked. He apologized. She cried. He ex-

plained. He begged. He pleaded. She considered, resolved, refused. He
stood. He clenched. He perspired. He spat. She flinched, paled.

He stopped. He slumped. He collapsed.

She stood. She pitied. She left.

They lived. They forgot. They died.

Because

Because everyone had said not to. Because the sunshine. Because the solitude. Because he felt invincible, though he understood that everyone who did the wrong thing felt invincible doing it. Knowing that made it better still, because he was part of something larger, the grand delusion of youth. Because the rock beneath his bare feet was hot, and the cold water below it roared as it met other water. Because the birds circled below him in the mist. Because he was already doing it and the water was rising to prove him right or wrong.

Ending

She and he are talking loudly, to be heard over the noise of the machines outside. The machines have been digging a hole in the street all day. She and he have been talking all day. They're looking for an ending. The machines are looking for a broken pipe. The water in the house is muddy. Which is why they called in the machines. She is calling him a liar and he is calling her bitch. The future is muddy and they are looking for an ending. Now they are screaming and the machines are screaming. Now they have found something. The machines stop. She and he stop. A sound reaches them from somewhere in the house, of air rising up through water, bursting out.

That's it. That's the ending.

Acknowledgments

Some of these stories appeared previously in the following periodicals and anthologies, sometimes in a different form:

The Arkansas International: "Circuit City"
Barrelhouse: "Let Me Think"
Better: "Husbands"
Bookanista: "Doors"
DIAGRAM: "Nine of Swords"
Epoch: "As Usual, Only the Crows," "By the Light of Small Explosions," "In Darkness," "Lost and Gone," "SuperAmerica," "Unnamed"
Gigantic Worlds: "Something You May Not Have Known about Vera"
Los Angeles Review: "The Deaths of Animals," "Jim's Eye"
The Louisville Review: "Marriage (Dogs)," "Marriage (Game)," "Marriage (Marriage)," "Marriage (Mystery)"
Marry a Monster: "Marriage (Pie)," "Marriage (Whiskey)"
Matchbook Stories: "Marriage (Fault)"
McSweeney's: "Pins," "Subject Verb"
Monkeybicycle: "Falling Down the Stairs"
The New Yorker: "Breadman," "The Loop"
Outlook Springs: "The Regulations"

Pie and Whiskey: *Writers under the Influence of Butter and Booze*:
   "Marriage (Divorce (Pie))"
Salon: "Apparently Not," "Monsters"
The Short Story Advent Calendar 2016: "Blue Light, Red Light"
The Short Story Advent Calendar 2019: "The Unsupported Circle"
Significant Objects: "Choirboy"
Slate: "The Museum of Near Misses"
Unstuck: "The Cottage on the Hill"
Willow Springs: "Eleven," "Marriage (Love)," "Marriage (Sick)," "Owl"

"Lipogram for a Passover Turkey Knife" was written in response to a
prompt from Magna Wonder-Knife Inc., of the Empire State Building,
New York, NY: "Here is my ten or more word statement as to WHY
THE MAGNA WONDER-KNIFE FOOD SLICER IS BEST."

"Boys" and "Girls" were written for a chapbook, *Boys≠Girls*, published by LunaSea Press, in Ithaca, New York, and presented at the
Spring Writes Literary Festival in May 2015.

"Falling Down the Stairs" and "It's Over" were originally written
for and performed at the Friday-night Merrill House readings at the
Colgate Writers Conference.

"Marriage (Pie)" and "Marriage (Whiskey)" were originally written for
and performed at the Pie & Whiskey Reading at the Montana Book
Festival in September 2015, in Missoula, Montana.

"The Museum of Near Misses" is a cover of Vladimir Nabokov's "The
Visit to the Museum."

J. Robert Lennon is the author of nine novels, including *Subdivision*, *Broken River*, and *Familiar*, and two other story collections, *Pieces for the Left Hand* and *See You in Paradise*. He lives in Ithaca, New York.

The text of *Let Me Think* is set in Adobe Garamond Pro. Book design by Ann Sudmeier. Composition by Bookmobile Design & Digital Publisher Services, Minneapolis, Minnesota. Manufactured by McNaughton & Gunn on acid-free, 100 percent postconsumer wastepaper.